SICILIAN'S
SHOCK
PROPOSAL

SICILIAN'S SHOCK PROPOSAL

BY

CAROL MARINELLI

MILLS & BOON

First published in Great Britain 2015
by Mills & Boon, an imprint of Harlequin (UK) Limited,
Large Print edition 2015
Eton House, 18-24 Paradise Road,
Richmond, Surrey, TW9 1SR

© 2015 Carol Marinelli

ISBN: 978-0-263-25696-3

Harlequin (UK) Limited's policy is to use papers that are natural, renewable and recyclable products and made from wood grown in sustainable forests. The logging and manufacturing processes conform to the legal environmental regulations of the country of origin.

Printed and bound in Great Britain
by CPI Antony Rowe, Chippenham, Wiltshire

PROLOGUE

'A WOMAN WHO says she's your fiancée is in Reception, asking to see you.'

Luka Cavaliere looked up from his computer and saw the wry smile on his PA's face.

'I thought I'd heard it all until now,' said Tara.

Women would try anything to get an audience with Luka, but to have someone pretending to be his fiancée was a first. Tara knew from bitter experience that the woman in Reception was lying—the only thing that Luka ever fully committed to was work.

She certainly wasn't expecting his response.

'Tell Reception that she can come up,' he said in his rich Italian voice.

'Sorry?'

Luka didn't respond to Tara's question. Instead, he got back to the work he was doing on his computer. Certainly he did not need to repeat himself to his PA, nor explain things to her.

'Luka?' Still Tara hovered at the door, unable to believe that he knew who this woman was—he hadn't even asked for her name.

'Do you want a second warning?' Luka checked. 'I have already told you that I should not have to give out my instructions twice.'

'No, you want to *give* me a second warning so that soon you can fire me.' Tara's voice was thick with tears. 'You want me gone…?'

Of course he did.

'It's because we made love, isn't it?' she simpered.

He could correct her but he chose not to. Luka didn't make love—he had sex.

Often.

His wealth attracted shallow women, but his dark good looks and skills in the bedroom did not lead to the fleeting encounters that he preferred. Always they wanted more than he was prepared to give. He knew that he should never have got involved with his latest PA, especially when he'd just trained her up to be useful.

'I'm not going to get into a discussion,' Luka said. 'Send her up.'

'But you never said that you were engaged. You never even gave a hint that there was anyone else—'

Bored now, Luka thought. 'Take as long as you like for lunch,' he interrupted. Yes, he wanted her gone. 'Actually, you can take the rest of the day off.'

Tara let out a hopeless sob and then turned and rather loudly left the office.

The slam of the door made Luka's eyes shut for a brief moment.

It had nothing to do with his PA's brief outburst, or the noise from the door—it was what would happen in the coming moments that he was bracing himself for.

There had *always* been someone else.

And now she was here.

He stood up from his desk and moved to the window and looked down below to the London street. It was the middle of summer—not that he usually noticed. His life was spent in air-conditioned comfort and he dressed in the same dark suits whatever the month.

It was ironic, Luka thought, that he and Sophie, after all these years, should meet in London—the place of their far younger dreams.

Until recently he had always assumed that if they did come face to face again it would be in Roma, perhaps on one of his regular visits there. Or even back in Bordo Del Cielo—the coastal town on Sicily's west coast where they had grown up. He had only returned once, for his father's funeral last year, but he had been wondering whether he might go back one final time if Sophie's father decided he wanted to be buried there.

Luka still hadn't made up his mind if, when that day came, he would attend the funeral.

He knew that that day was coming soon.

And that, he also knew, was the reason that Sophie was here.

His hand reached into his jacket and he took

out not a photo, not a memory; instead, it was a brutal reminder as to why they could never be.

He stared at the thin gold chain that wrapped around his long fingers and then he looked at the simple gold cross that lay in his palm. Yes, he would go to her father's funeral, for this necklace belonged in that grave.

It took only a few moments for Sophie to make her way from the foyer to his suite yet it felt like for ever as he awaited her arrival, but then came the knock at the door that he recognised from yesteryear.

How much easier might his life have been had he not answered the door that long-ago day? Perhaps, Luka thought, he should not respond to it now.

He pocketed the necklace and cleared his throat. 'Come in.' He managed a deep summons but, as the door opened, he did not turn around.

'Your assistant asked me to pass on the message that she's just resigned. Apparently I'm the final straw.'

The sound of her voice, though a touch stilted

and measured, still held, for Luka, the same caress.

For a man who feared little, he was nervous to turn around.

Luka rather hoped that the years that had passed since they'd last met had not treated her kindly—he fleetingly hoped that a nice little drug habit might have aged her terribly, or that she was pregnant with triplets perhaps...anything that might douse the eternal flame.

He turned and found out that time had indeed been cruel, to him at least, for perfection greeted his navy eyes.

Sophie Durante stood before him again.

She was wearing a simple dress in the palest ivory that showed her curvaceous figure. Her glossy, long black hair was worn neatly up in a French roll when he remembered it spilling over naked shoulders.

Her neutral-coloured high-heeled shoes enhanced her toned olive legs.

He forced his gaze up but only made it as far as her mouth. Her full lips were pressed tightly together when he remembered them once laughing and smiling. Then he remembered them somewhere else, which was a rather inconvenient image to have sprung to mind, so he forced himself to meet those dark brown eyes again.

She was just as beautiful as he remembered and, just as they had at their parting, her eyes showed she abhorred him.

Luka stared back with mutual loathing.

'Sophie.' He gave her a curt nod.

He did not know how he should greet her—shake her hand, or kiss both cheeks perhaps?

Instead, he gestured for her to take a seat.

She did so; placing her designer bag by the seat, she neatly crossed her legs at the ankles.

'You look well,' Luka said, and hoped she might miss that he then cleared his throat—for those first delicate traces of her scent had now reached him and his mind was firing taunting glimpses of memory.

'I am well,' she responded, and gave him a tight smile. 'I am very busy, of course.'

'Are you working?' Luka asked. 'Did you ever get to work on the ships?'

'No.' Sophie shook her head. 'I am an events planner.'

'Really?' He didn't even attempt to hide his surprise. 'You were always running late for everything.'

He glanced at the ring on her finger—a ruby stone set in Italian gold. It was very old-fashioned and far from what he would have chosen for her. 'I have terrible taste in rings, it would seem,' Luka said.

'Don't!' she warned abruptly. 'You will never insult me again.'

He looked up and into the eyes of the only woman he had ever made love to as she asked him a question.

'Aren't you going to ask why I am here?'

'I presume you're about to tell me.' Luka shrugged. He knew damn well why she was here but he'd make her say it just for the pleasure of watching her squirm.

'My father may be released from prison this Friday on compassionate grounds.'

'I know that.'

'How?'

'I do occasionally glance at the news.' Luka's sarcasm didn't garner a response, though his voice was kinder when he asked her a question. 'How is he doing?'

'Don't pretend that you care.'

'And don't *dare* assume that I don't!' he snapped, and he watched her rapid blink as he continued speaking.

Seeing her, he had been momentarily side-swiped but now he took back control and made a vow never to lose his control with her again.

'But, then, that's you all over, Sophie. Your mind was always made up even before the jury had been chosen. I'll ask you again. How is your father?'

'He is fading, he is a little confused at times.'

'I'm sorry to hear that.'

'Isn't that what prison does to an innocent man?'

Luka stared back and for now said nothing.

Paulo was not as innocent as Sophie made out.

'Not that a Cavaliere would know about prison,' she added.

'I spent six months in prison awaiting trial, two of them in solitary,' Luka pointed out. 'Or were you referring to my father being found not guilty?'

'I have no wish to discuss that man.' She couldn't, Luka noted, even bring herself to say his father's name. How much worse would this conversation be if she knew the truth? he wondered. He could almost feel the heat from the necklace in his pocket. He was actually tempted to toss it across the desk to her, to end them once and for all.

'Just what are you doing here, Sophie? I thought we ended our engagement a long time ago.'

'Firstly, I don't want you to think, for even a moment, that I am here for any romantic reasons.'

'Good, because it would be an extremely wasted journey if that were the case.'

'However,' she continued, 'my father believes

that you upheld your promise. He thinks we got engaged and that we now live together in Rome.'

'Why would Paulo think that?'

'It was kinder to lie and let him think that you upheld your commitment to me. I never thought he would be let out and now that he might be I need to keep up the pretence. I told him that the terrible things you said in court about me were in an attempt to protect him.'

'They were,' Luka responded. 'I said what I did in the hope of protecting him, or rather protecting you. You simply refused to see it from my side.' He looked at her for a very long moment and found he could not stand even having her in the same room so he shook his head. 'It wouldn't work.'

'It *has* to work,' Sophie said. 'You owe me.'

'I do.' Luka did not concede with those words. He knew she spoke the truth. 'But apart from the fact that neither of us can abide being in the same room together, I do have a life. I might be seeing someone...'

'I don't care if this upends your life for a while.

This is going to happen, Luka. You might sit a rich man in your posh London office and live a jet-set lifestyle but you are *from* Bordo Del Cielo, you cannot escape from that. You might go through women like tissues but the fact remains we were promised to each other from childhood and where we come from that means something.' Luka let out a tense breath as she asked again. 'Will you help my father die in peace?'

'You want me to move in with you and pretend that we live together?'

'No, I read that you have an apartment in Rome...we will use that.'

'Why not yours?'

'I share with my friend Bella. You might remember her...'

Luka bit back a sarcastic response. From what he had heard, a *lot* of men might remember Bella!

'She runs a business from our home.'

As she spoke, he noted that Sophie ignored his slight sardonic smile, even though she must know what it insinuated.

'It would not be fair to disrupt Bella and it

would look odd for us, as a couple, to be sharing a home with her.'

'And would this loving couple be sharing a bed?' He voiced the obvious question but she did not answer directly.

'It would look strange for us to sleep apart.'

'Would there be sex?' he asked, wishing a blush would rise on her cheeks, for Sophie to give some indication that this hurt like hell for her also, but she stared back coolly as she delivered her response.

'I would think not,' she said. 'Since that evening, given what happened, I have a phobia...'

Luka's eyes widened. Was Sophie saying that there had been no one since him? There was a small rush of giddy relief that he quickly doused but she hadn't finished speaking. 'But if that is what it will take for you to agree, then, yes, there can be sex.'

'I thought Bella was the whore.'

'We can all be whores,' Sophie responded with spite, and Luka looked at the beautiful yet hostile stranger whose innocence he had taken, never to return. 'So, yes, if sex is to be part of the deal—'

'No, thanks,' Luka interrupted. 'I don't need charity sex and, anyway, martyrs don't turn me on—it's extremely willing participants that do.' He watched the slight swallow in her neck and he knew, he just knew she was remembering how good they had been so he cruelly walked her down memory lane and, as he did so, he reinforced a truth. 'Surely you know how much I like a woman who instigates things.'

He'd thought she'd blush as he pointed out how she had been the one who had practically begged him to make love to her yet, rather than blush, Sophie surprised him with a shrug and a smile.

'Well, there will be no sex for us, then, because I won't be instigating anything. Are you going to do this, Luka?'

'I'd like some time to think about it.'

'My father doesn't have time.'

'Leave me your business card, Sophie, I'll call you when I've made up my mind.'

He watched as she went into her bag and for the first time appeared flustered. 'I don't have any with me.'

'Give me your number.'

'I will contact you.' Sophie stood and went to leave but at the last moment changed her mind. 'You owe me this, Luka, we were promised to each other. You took my virginity.'

He could only admire her for, unlike most women, she spoke of their time together without misty recall. In fact, she reduced it to cold fact.

Almost.

'Took?' he checked. 'What an odd choice of word. You see, from my recollection...' Now a blush spread from her neck and rose to her cheeks. He came around the desk and stood in front of her, and she backed up to the desk. 'Are you going to jump up, Sophie...or do your prefer a kitchen bench to an office desk?'

Now she was struggling to keep her cool.

'Why didn't I marry you?' He played devil's advocate. 'You being such a good Sicilian girl...'

'I told my father that it was my dream for him to walk me down the aisle. I told him—'

'Stop there,' Luka interrupted. 'I need to think about what I'm prepared to agree to but before we go any further there is something that you need to know.' They were face to face as he said it. 'I will *never* marry you.'

'You'll do whatever it takes.' The spitfire he had known was returning and she jabbed a finger into his chest to make her point. 'Whatever. It. Takes.'

'No,' he calmly interrupted. Despite the cool facade she had attempted, he knew that she was as Sicilian as the volcanic soil they were from, and as he watched her struggle to hold in her temper, he didn't suppress his slight triumphant smile. She was just as volatile and passionate as he remembered. Those traits in Sophie were everything he both loved and loathed.

'After what you did, after what you said about me in court…'

'Lose the drama, Sophie,' His voice was completely calm. 'I accept that I have a moral debt to you, given all that happened, but, even with several years' interest added, I do not owe you that much. I will agree to be your fake fiancé, but never your fake husband. Know that now, or get the hell out.'

He hoped for the latter. Get the hell out of my life, my head, my heart.

Just get out!

Instead, Sophie must have accepted his terms for she sat back down.

It was time to talk business.

Finally, together, they would face the mistakes of their past.

CHAPTER ONE

'HAPPY BIRTHDAY FOR TOMORROW!'

Sophie smiled as Bella went into her bag and bought out a neatly wrapped package.

'Can I open it now?' Sophie asked. She already knew what it was—a dress for her engagement party next week. Even though they worked as chambermaids, Bella was a talented dressmaker and Sophie had spent the last few weeks having sheets of paper pinned to her. She couldn't wait to see the real thing. Bella had kept it a complete surprise and Sophie didn't even know what colour the dress was.

'Don't open it here.' Bella shook her head. 'Wait till you get home. You don't want to get sand on it.'

Though tired from the shifts as chambermaids at the Brezza Oceana hotel, just as they always did they had come to their secret cove. It wasn't really a secret cove but it was tucked behind jagged cliffs and could not be seen from the hotel. The tourists didn't really know about it as the small beach was accessible by a path that the locals of Bordo Del Cielo kept to themselves. When the hotel had first been built, much to the locals' disgust, it was here that Sophie and Bella would come after school. Now, even though they worked together most days, still the tradition remained.

Here, where no one might overhear them, they came and sat, their legs dangling in the azure water, chatting about their hopes and dreams and voicing some of their fears...

Not all of their fears, though.

Bordo Del Cielo was a town of secrets and some things were too dangerous for even the closest of friends to discuss.

'Now I can get on with making my own dress,' Bella said.

'What is yours like?'

'Grey,' Bella replied. 'Very simple, very sophisticated. Maybe then Matteo might notice me...'

Sophie laughed. Matteo was Luka's best friend and had been Bella's crush for years, but he had never given her so much as a glance.

'You must be getting excited,' Bella said, and Sophie was about to smile and nod.

In fact, she did so.

'Of course I am,' she said, but her smile, the one she had worn so determinedly whenever her upcoming engagement was discussed, suddenly wavered and rare tears started to fill her expressive brown eyes.

'Sophie?' Bella checked when she saw that her friend was struggling. 'Tell me.'

'I can't.'

'Are you worried about...?' Bella hesitated. 'Sleeping with him? I know he might expect you to once you are engaged but you could tell Luka that you are a good girl and want to wait for your wedding night.'

Sophie actually managed a small laugh. 'That's the only part I'm not worried about.'

It was the truth.

Oh, she hadn't seen Luka in years but she had grown up nursing a crush on him. Luka's widowed father was rich; Malvolio owned the hotel and most of the businesses and homes in town. Those Malvolio didn't own he took payments from for their protection. When Luka's mother had died, instead of struggling to raise his child, in the way Sophie's father had, Malvolio had sent Luka away. He had attended boarding school on the mainland but, every summer when he'd returned, to Sophie he'd looked more beautiful. She had no doubt that the years he had spent in London wouldn't have dimmed that.

'I'm actually looking forward to seeing Luka again.'

'Remember how you cried when he left?'

'I was fourteen then,' Sophie said. 'Tomorrow I'll be nineteen…'

'Do you remember when you tried to kiss him?' Bella laughed and Sophie cringed in recall.

'He told me I was too young. I guess he would have been twenty then.' She smiled at the embarrassing memory of Luka dropping her from his lap. 'He told me to wait.'

'And you have.'

'He hasn't, though,' Sophie said, her voice bitter. Luka's reputation was as undeniable as the waves that pulled at their calves. 'He didn't back then, he was already screwing around.'

'Does it make you angry?'

'Yes, but more...' She felt a familiar burn rise in her chest—little bubbles of jealousy at the thought of Luka with other women that did not ease when they popped, for it felt like shards of glass were being released in her throat. 'I want what he has had.'

'You want to date other men?'

'No, I want my freedom,' Sophie said. 'I want to have experiences and chase my own dreams. I've spent my life taking care of my father's home, cooking his meals, doing his washing. I don't know if I want to be someone's wife yet. I want to work on the cruise liners...' She looked out to the sparkling ocean. Travelling, sailing on the seas had always been her dream. 'I wouldn't mind making beds for a living if I could do it on a ship. It's like you with your dressmaking...'

'That's just a dream, though,' Bella said.

'Perhaps not. Your application might be accepted. You might be off to Milan soon.'

'I got rejected,' Bella said. 'My drawings weren't enough for them and I'll never be able to afford models and photographers for a decent portfolio.' Bella shrugged her shoulders as she both tried and failed to convince Sophie that not getting in to study fashion design in Milan didn't hurt like hell. 'I could never have gone anyway. I need my wage to pay the rent. Malvolio would give my mother hell if...' Bella's voice trailed off and she shook her head.

Yes, there were things that should never be discussed, but with her engagement now less than a week away Sophie could no longer keep her fears in. 'I don't want to be pulled even closer into Malvolio's life. I don't think Luka is anything like his father but—'

'Shh,' Bella said, and even though they had the

cove to themselves she looked over both shoulders just to make sure. 'Don't speak like that.'

'Why not?' Sophie pushed. 'We're just friends talking.'

Bella said nothing.

'I don't want to get married.'

There—Sophie had said it.

'I'll be barely nineteen. There are so many things I want to do before I settle down. I don't know if I want to...'

'You don't know if you want to live with Luka in a beautiful home and be taken care of?' Bella's response was one of anger. 'You don't know if you want to be rich and pampered?' Bella was starting to shout. 'Well, I'd take it if I were you and count yourself lucky—after your engagement party Malvolio has told me to stay back. I'll be working the bar. This time next week I won't be making beds at the hotel, I'll be...' Bella broke down then and Sophie held her own tears in check. 'Like mother, like daughter,' Bella sobbed. 'I am not ashamed of my mother, she did what she had to to survive, but I don't want that for me.'

'Then don't do it!' Sophie shook her head furiously. 'You are to tell him no!'

'Do you think for a moment that he'd listen?'

'You don't have to jump to his rules. He can't make you do anything that you don't want to.' Sophie was insistent. She loathed the way everyone jumped at Malvolio's command, her own father included. 'If you can't say no to Malvolio then I shall for you.'

'Just leave it,' Bella pleaded.

'No, I will not leave it. When Luka gets here on Wednesday I'll try speaking with him…'

'It won't do anything.' Bella shook her head and stood. 'I need to get back…'

They walked down the little pathway together and Bella apologised for her outburst. 'I didn't mean to be cross with you. I understand that it should be your choice if you marry.'

'We should both have choices,' Sophie said.

They didn't, though.

Everyone considered Sophie lucky—that, because of her father's connections to Malvolio, she would marry Luka.

There had been no discussion with the future bride.

They came out of the trees and onto the hilly street and walked past the hotel Brezza Oceana, where Sophie and Luka's engagement party would be held.

'Are you taking your Pill?' Bella asked, because they had taken the bus two weeks ago to a neighboring town so that Sophie could get contraception without the local doctor knowing.

'Every day.'

'I'd better get some,' Bella said, and Sophie's heart twisted at the resignation in her friend's voice.

'Bella—'

'I have to go.'

'Will I see you tonight at church?'

'Of course.' Bella attempted a smile. 'I want to know if you like your dress.'

They parted ways and Sophie was almost home when she remembered she was supposed to have stopped for bread, so she turned and raced back to the deli.

As she walked in, the conversation stopped abruptly, just as it often did these days.

Sophie did her best to ignore the strange tension and when it was her turn she smiled at Teresa, the owner, and ordered the olives and cheese she had chosen, as well as a large pane Siciliano, which was surely the nicest bread in the world, and then took out her purse to pay.

'*Gratuitamente.*' Teresa told Sophie there would be no charge.

'*Scusi?*' Sophie frowned and then blushed. She was being let off paying because she was marrying Malvoio's son, Sophie decided. Well, she wanted no part in that sort of thing and angrily she took out some money, placed it on the counter and then walked out.

'You're late,' Paulo said, when Sophie let herself into their home and walked through to the kitchen, where her father was sitting reading his paper at the table. 'You would be late for your own funeral.'

'Bella and I got talking,' Sophie said.

'What do you have there?'

'Just some bread and olives...' Sophie answered, and then realised that he was referring to the parcel she was carrying, but before she explained what it was she asked her father a question. 'Father, when I went to pay, Teresa said there was no charge. Why would she say that?'

'I don't know.' Paulo shrugged. 'Perhaps she was being nice. After all, you are there every day.'

'No.' Sophie refused to be fobbed off. 'It was uncomfortable when I walked in—everyone stopped talking. I think it might have something to do with my getting engaged to Luka.'

'What is in the parcel?' Her father changed the subject and Sophie let out a tense breath as she set down the food and pulled out some plates.

'Bella gave me my birthday present a day early. It's my dress for my engagement. I'm going to try it on when I have had my shower. Father...' As she cut up the loaf Sophie did her best to sound casual. 'You remember you said I could have my mother's jewellery when I got engaged?'

'I said that you could have it when you got married.'

'No!' Sophie corrected. 'You told me years ago that I could have it when Luka and I got engaged. Can I have them now, please? I want to see how my dress looks with everything.'

'Sophie I've just sat down...'

'Then I will fetch them if you tell me where they are.'

Her father let out a sigh of relief as the phone rang and, though not prepared to get her mother's jewellery, he happily headed out to answer the phone.

He was always making excuses. For years Sophie had been asking for her mother's necklace and earrings and always he came up with different reason why she couldn't have them yet.

'Father...' she started as he came back into the kitchen.

'Not now, Sophie. Malvolio has called a meeting.'

'But it's Sunday,' Sophie said.

'He said that there is something important that needs to be discussed.'

'Well, surely it can wait till Monday?'

'Enough, Sophie,' her father snapped. 'It is not for me to question him.'

'Why not?' Sophie challenged. She was sick and tired of her father being Malvolio's puppet. 'What is this *meeting* about? Or is it just an excuse to sit in the bar for the evening?'

Surprisingly, her father laughed. 'You sound just like your mother.'

Everyone said the same. Rosa had had fire apparently, not that Sophie could remember her as she had died when Sophie was two.

'Here,' Paulo said, and handed her a small pouch. 'These are her jewels.'

Sophie let out a small gasp and then looked at her father and saw that he was sweating and a little grey.

'This means so much.'

'I know,' Paulo said, his voice shaken. 'There are only her earrings.'

'I thought there was a necklace...' In all the

photos Rosa wore a simple gold cross but she could hear the emotion in her father's voice when he told her that he didn't have it.

'It was a very fine chain. I believe that it came off in the accident. Even after all these years I still look for it in the bushes when I take my walk in the morning. I wanted you to have it. I'm so sorry that I cannot give that to you.'

'Is that why you haven't let me have them?' Sophie asked. 'Father, I just wanted something... anything of hers...' She looked at the fine gold hoops, that had a small diamond in each, with tears in her eyes. 'And now I have her earrings. Thank you so much.'

'I have to go to my meeting,' Paulo said, and Sophie pressed her lips together. She didn't want to fight, especially not when he had just given her something so precious, but her father looked terrible and she really did want him to rest. 'I'll try and get back for dinner.'

Sophie simply could not hold her tongue. 'If Malvolio lets you.'

She saw her father's eyes shut for a brief moment before he turned and headed for the door.

Sophie knew it might be kinder to apologise and that she was maybe making things harder for her father by admitting her truth but she didn't like his involvement with Malvolio.

'Father, I don't know if I am ready to get engaged...' She held her breath as her father's shoulders stiffened.

'It is normal to be nervous,' her father said, but did not turn around. 'Sophie, I have to go.'

'Father, please, can we talk...?'

But the door had already closed.

Sophie walked around the small home and picked up a picture of her mother. She could see the similarities there—they had the same long black hair, the same dark brown eyes and full lips. Oh, Sophie wished she was here, just for a moment. She missed having a mother to give her advice so badly.

'I am so confused,' Sophie admitted to the photo of Rosa. A part of her dreaded being married, yet there was another part of her that longed to see Luka again, the man who had always filled her dreams. She had always looked up to him, had always nursed a crush on him, and she wanted her first kiss to belong to them and to be made love to by Luka.

What would Luka want, though?

She blushed in embarrassment at the thought of him returning and being forced to marry her.

No doubt he was dreading next weekend and returning to uphold his father's commitment for him to marry poor little Sophie Durante.

Was that the hold Malvolio had over her father? Sophie wondered.

Well, she didn't need charity and she would tell her father that.

She put down the photo, took her parcel upstairs and finally opened it.

The dress was exquisite. It was in the softest chiffon and the colour was a very pale coral. Sophie badly wanted to try it on but she had a very quick shower and washed her hair and then combed it before picking up the dress.

She slipped it over her head and looked in the mirror.

Sophie found she was holding her breath. All those hours standing as Bella had pinned sheets of paper had been worth it for this moment.

The dress was amazing. It was scooped low at the front and showed Sophie's cleavage. Of course, it would need a bra but even without it was somehow both elegant and sexy. It came in at the waist and then fell in layers, emphasising her curves when usually Sophie did what she could to downplay them.

Yes, she knew she should take it off but instead she put on her mother's earrings and found the lip glaze she had bought.

Working at the hotel, Sophie was used to seeing beautiful women but this afternoon, for the first time in her life, she felt like one.

Now she blushed for different reasons when she imagined facing Luka.

She wanted him to see her grown up.

Briefly she imagined his mouth on hers but a

loud knocking on the door snapped her out of her daydream.

It sounded urgent and Sophie ran through the house but she smiled when she opened the door and saw that it was just Pino on his bike.

He was twelve years old and everyone used him as a messenger.

'Malvolio wants you to go to his home,' Pino said in a self-important voice.

'Malvolio.' Sophie frowned. She had never been to Malvolio's home. 'Why? What does he want?'

'I was just told to give you the message,' Pino said, balancing on his bike. 'He said that it is important and that you're to go there now.'

Sophie went and got Pino some money and thanked him but her heart was racing.

Why would Malvolio ask her to go to his home?

She had assumed that he and her father were meeting at the hotel bar.

Sophie thought of her father's grey complexion and the sweat on his face and was suddenly worried that he might have been taken ill.

She slipped on some sandals and ran up the hill towards Malvolio's spectacular home, which overlooked not just the ocean but the entire town. Once there she took a breath and then knocked on the door. She didn't want to be there but he had summoned her after all.

No one ever said no to Malvolio.

CHAPTER TWO

'WHY DON'T YOU ask Sophie to come over?'

Luka let out a tense breath at his father's suggestion. Against his father's wishes he had been in London for the last six years, at first studying but now he was now starting to make a name for himself.

He had offered some financial advice to a boutique hotel, but when unable to pay him to implement the changes Luka had offered to work for them for a stake in the hotel.

It had been a gamble. For a year he had worked for nothing by day and earned money by working in a bar at night.

Now, though, the hotel was starting to flourish and Luka owned ten percent of a thriving business.

Luka had his start.

He could have it all here, he knew that.

His father was one of the wealthiest men in Sicily, and he should be stepping in now. His father thought he was back to settle down and start taking over his empire, but instead Luka was choosing to step out for good.

His time away had opened his eyes. With an increasing awareness of his father's corrupt ways he had chosen to stay away and had made only the occasional trip home to Sicily.

Deliberately he hadn't seen or spoken to Sophie in that time.

And in that time an awful lot had changed.

'It might be nice to spend some time with her before the engagement party,' Malvolio pushed. 'Angela will be at church all day and I know that there is a bible meeting this evening she wants to attend,' he said, referring to their maid. 'I'll go out and give you two some time—'

'There isn't going to be an engagement party,' Luka said, and met the eyes of his father—a man who he did not even recognise, for Luka had come to understand that he had never really known his father at all. 'Because there isn't going to be an engagement. I'm not marrying Sophie Durante.'

'But the two of you have been promised to each other since childhood.'

'That was your promise, not mine,' Luka said. 'You chose my future wife, the same way you have chosen for me to follow in the family business. I'm here to tell you that I am going to be returning to London. I'm not going to live and work here.'

'You can't do that to Paulo, to Sophie.'

'Don't pretend you care about them,' Luka said, and watched his father start to breathe harder as he realised the challenge he was facing.

'I won't let you do it to me,' Malvolio said. 'You will not shame the Cavaliere name.'

Luka jaw gritted. His father had no shame. His father took from the poor, from the sick, his father ruled the people of Bordo Del Cielo with an iron fist—*there* was the real shame.

'I will speak with Sophie's father and explain that I will not have a bride chosen for me. The same way that I will not have my career, nor the place on this planet where I live, dictated to me.'

'You will destroy Sophie's reputation.'

'I am not discussing this,' Luka said. 'I am telling you that I shall speak with Paulo about my decision and then, if he will allow me to, I will talk to Sophie myself.'

'You are not returning to London, you will work with me. After all I have done for you—'

'Don't!' Luka said. 'Don't say that you did all this for me when I never asked for any of it.'

'But you took,' Malvolio said. 'You have lived in the best home and I gave you the very best education. I have a business waiting for you to take over. I will not let you walk out on that.'

'Let me?' Luka checked. 'It's not for you to choose how I live. I don't need your permission for anything.' He went to walk off but his father stopped him in the way he knew best.

Luka, at twenty-four, could have halted the punch that was coming to him but he did not. His father sent him crashing back into the wall and there was a gush of warm blood down his face. Not that it would stop Malvolio.

His only son, his only child was now turning his back on everything Malvolio had worked for and Luka had known that it would come to this.

Too often, growing up, it had.

As his head hit the wall his father thumped him in the stomach and as Luka doubled over Malvolio's fist came into his ribs, but all it did was reaffirm to Luka that his decision to leave for good was the right one.

While he did not hit his father, Luka pulled himself back to his feet and faced him. 'Clever men fight with their minds,' Luka said, as Malvolio raised his fist again. 'Whereas you instil fear...' He shrugged his father off. 'But not in me. The next punch you deliver will be returned,' he warned—and he meant it.

'You will marry her.'

Luka might not have fought back but anger raged through his veins. He loathed his father's assumptions and the way he dictated his life, and he told him so.

'I live in London,' he shouted. 'I date models now, glamorous, sophisticated women, not some peasant that you have chosen for me.'

'I have to go to a meeting,' Malvolio hissed. 'We will speak of this when I return.'

Luka said nothing, standing bruised and bleeding and a bit breathless as his father picked up his car keys and stormed out.

He headed up to his old bedroom and stripped off his shirt then went into his bathroom and examined the damage.

There was bruising to his ribcage and on his shoulder where it had met the wall. An old gash above his eyes had opened up and probably needed stitching.

Not now, though.

For now he would patch himself up and then head to the airport. He might call Matteo and ask if he wanted to meet for a drink but they would meet at the airport.

He was done with Bordo Del Cielo.

Sophie.

As he splashed cold water on his face he thought of her.

Yes, this would be hell for her, Luka knew that and it didn't sit right with him. Perhaps before he left for good he should go and speak with Paulo and maybe Sophie too.

He pressed his bloodied shirt over his eye and went into his suitcase to find a fresh one. He hadn't unpacked. Luka hadn't even been back home for an hour before the argument had started.

He heard a knock at the door but ignored it.

Angela could get it, but then he remembered that she was at church.

There was another knock but more loudly this time, and Luka headed down the stairs and opened the door.

The breath that had just returned after his father had knocked it out of him stilled inside Luka now.

His voice, when it finally came, was low and curious, and even though he said but one word there was a slight huskiness.

'Sophie?'

He was struggling to meet her eyes. In the argument that had just taken place, as he had attempted to wrestle back his life from his father's control, things had been said about Sophie.

Things she did not deserve.

It had been said in the heat of the moment. Vile words in a vile row and Luka could taste bitterness along with blood in his mouth.

Now, though, as finally he looked at her, there was a pleasant silence. No other thoughts other than this moment.

Her eyes were the same, yet more knowing. Her mouth was full and she was wearing a little make-up.

Her hair was thicker and longer.

And her body—he could not help but briefly look down. The skinny teenager he remembered had left and in her place stood a very beautiful woman.

One whose heart he was about to break.

CHAPTER THREE

'LUKA?' SOPHIE FROWNED. 'I didn't think you were getting here till Wednesday.'

'There was a change of plan.'

'What happened?' Sophie asked.

'I decided to fly home earlier—'

'I meant to your face.'

'It's just a cut,' Luka said. 'An old cut that opened up.'

'The bruises are new,' Sophie pointed out, and he gave a pale smile.

'My father,' he admitted.

Sophie didn't really know what to say to that so she cleared her throat and got back to the reason she was standing at the door.

'I just had a message from Pino. Your father said I was to come here. That it was important.'

'I can guess why,' Luka said. No doubt his father had thought that one look at Sophie and he would change his mind. Well, he wasn't that shallow. He saw her frown as he explained things a little better. 'I think my father wanted us to be alone.'

'Oh.'

'You know how manipulative he can be,' Luka said.

She didn't answer. Everyone might think that of Malvolio but no one would ever dare to say it.

'Come in, Sophie.' He held open the door and after a moment's hesitation she stepped inside. 'We need to talk.' She followed him through to the kitchen, her eyes taking in his back and wide shoulders, and she felt very small and not in a nice way.

He was so glossy, so sophisticated, he was everything that she wasn't.

Of course he wouldn't want her.

And now, from the little he had said, and the way he couldn't quite meet her eyes, Sophie guessed she was about to be told that.

Yes, she had her doubts about the engagement—yes, she wasn't sure if she wanted to get married—but it felt very different from being told to your face that you weren't wanted.

'I just need to sort out this cut,' Luka said. 'Take a seat.'

She didn't.

'I don't know where Angela keeps the first-aid kit,' Luka continued as he went through the cupboards. 'Here it is.' Sophie watched as he pulled out a small first-aid kit and even smiled as his long fingers tried to open a sticking plaster while holding the shirt over his eye.

'It needs more than a plaster,' Sophie said. 'You need a doctor to stitch it.'

'I'll get it sutured tomorrow if it needs it,' Luka said. 'In London.'

He looked up and caught her eye but she didn't respond to his opening.

She'd damn well make him say it, Sophie decided.

'I'll do it,' Sophie said, because it really was a nasty cut. She took out the scissors then cut the sticking plaster into thin strips onto the kitchen bench, and as she did so Luka spoke.

'You look well.'

Sophie gave a wry smile. At least he had got to see her in her beautiful dress, she thought with slight relish. She knew she looked her very best and it was a rather nice thing to know when you were about to be dumped.

Let him think she ran around on a Sunday in coral chiffon with lip gloss and jewellery...

And no underwear, Sophie remembered, as she jumped up onto the kitchen bench and quickly put her dress between her thighs.

'Come here,' Sophie said, now that she had set up for the small procedure.

'I don't want to get blood on your dress.'

It didn't matter now if her dress was ruined, Sophie knew. This was the only time that he'd be seeing her in it. 'Oh, this old thing.' She shrugged. 'Don't worry about it.'

Luka went over to where she sat and stood as Sophie concentrated on closing the cut.

'Why were you two fighting?'

'We weren't fighting,' Luka said. 'He was taking out his temper on me. I chose not to hit him back. This one last time.'

'I hate how he treats you,' Sophie said, and her hand paused over the cut as she deliberated with herself whether or not to continue. 'How he treats everyone.'

She thought of Bella and if there was any good that could come out of this then she'd damn well find it.

'Bella's mother is sick,' Sophie said. 'She can't work and now he wants Bella to start doing shifts at the hotel bar.' She assumed, given that his eyes refused to meet hers, that he knew what that meant. 'Can you speak with him for me?'

'Sophie, before we discuss Bella I need to speak first with you.'

'I get that you do,' she said, 'but I would like to speak about this first'. Sophie persisted because she knew she might lose her temper about five minutes from now. Yes, she didn't want to be forced into a marriage but, no, she didn't want to be left here either.

It wasn't just her pride that was going to hurt when he ended things—now that he was back her heart remembered him.

Standing before her was the man she had cried herself to sleep over when he had left last time.

It had been a childish crush, a schoolgirl's dream, a teenage fantasy, Sophie's head knew that but, having him back, feeling him close, her heart was racing again and her body wanted to taste first-hand her forbidden dreams. Yes, soon that Sicilian temper might get the best of her, so she would speak with him now, about the things that possibly could be sorted, while there was relative calm.

Relative, for her legs ached to wrap around him and the tongue that went over her lips now was inadvertently preparing herself for him. 'Bella doesn't want to work in the bar.'

She could sense his discomfort and guessed that it had little to do with the pain from the cut, more the subject matter.

'I'll speak to him,' Luka offered, 'but first I

need to speak with you. I was going to go and
see Paulo—'

'Luka...' Her hand was on his cheek and she
wanted to halt him, wanted to kiss him, to make
love and then deal with the rest.

Please, don't say it, she wanted to beg.

Not yet, not until I have finally tasted you.

'Luka, I know this is difficult but...'

She was right. Luka was not looking forward
to this conversation one bit. He wondered how
best he could tell her his reasoning without de-
stroying her belief in her father.

It was also difficult for other reasons.

Yes, Malvolio was a manipulative bastard and
Luka knew that he wasn't shallow enough to
change his mind just because Sophie looked sen-
sational. Still, it was rather hard to stand there at
eye level with the ripe swell of her breasts, with
the warm, musky scent of her reaching into him
and then to look into eyes that, Luka realised,
knew him.

Perhaps their fathers had chosen more wisely
than he had given them credit for, because the

ache in his groin and the surprising pleasure of talking to her had momentarily upended his plans.

He had to go through with it, Luka knew.

He had to deny the attraction, the want that was there between them.

Her pupils were large with lust, and he was sure that so too were his as they stared back to her. How the hell did you tell someone it was over when you were hard for them? When you knew, just knew, that with one slip of your hand those gorgeous thighs would part?

He needed to tell her they were over now, right now, before he gave in to the kiss they both wanted, and so he spoke on. 'My father was angry because I told him I wouldn't be coming back to Bordo Del Cielo and instead I would be living permanently in London. I told him I wanted no part of his life. I said that I won't have him choose where I live, how I work—'

'Don't I get a say in where we live?' Sophie said, refusing to make this easy for him.

She wanted to slap him.

Now that he was here, she wanted not just her dreams of freedom and working on the ships, she wanted him too.

Luka, who had swum in the river with her, Luka, who had told her the night he'd left her aching to be kissed by him that she must wait. He had been twenty years old when he had prised her off his lap and she had clung to him like glue.

She wanted the kiss that he had promised her then.

Instead, she finished closing his wound and then put a large plaster over the top as she spoke. 'My father will be upset. He always thought that I would live close to him and that our children would grow up in Bordo Del Cielo.'

Don't do this, she wanted to warn, though she knew that he was right to.

'In my time away, I've come to understand things.' Luka ran a tongue over tense lips as he reminded himself that he was going to do this without criticising her father. 'The way my father conducts business, the way my mother used to turn a blind eye to terrible deeds...' She looked at that beautiful mouth in his unshaven jaw and he confirmed her darkest thoughts. Malvolio was pure evil. 'I don't want any part of it,' Luka said.

'I don't like the hold he has on my father,' Sophie admitted. 'I don't think my father...' She couldn't bring herself to say it but she tried. 'I think some of my father's dealings are also wrong.'

'That's his choice,' Luka said. 'And I am making my own. I don't think that a promise our fathers made on our behalf should be something we feel we have to adhere to. I think we should be able to date and fall in love with whoever we choose.'

'And have you been dating?' Sophie asked, and Luka said nothing. 'Because if you have then it doesn't seem very fair when I have kept myself for you. I haven't so much as kissed another man, even though I have wanted to.' That was a lie, she'd never want another man. She had only ever wanted him. 'I have been to dances and parties and nothing, *nothing* has ever happened.'

Luka remained silent and Sophie assumed then that he was serious about someone.

'Is *she* insisting we break up?' The jealousy in her voice was not faked. Sophie's skin prickled at the thought of him with another woman.

'There is no *one* she,' Luka said. 'I have not been serious about any one person in particular, but...'

'You have been dating?'

'Yes.'

'You've kissed, made love...' all the things she had guessed he would be doing, all the things she had wanted Luka to do with her '...while all the time you were promised to me.'

Her hand came up then and he would have accepted a slap to the cheek but, hell, he'd just got the wound closed so he caught her wrist.

'You still have good reflexes,' Sophie said, because she had watched him play sport, catch a fork, grab her arm before she fell...

Luka frowned at the light tone to her voice and turned his attention from the wrist he was still holding and then saw that she was smiling.

'Sophie?'

'Perhaps I am not best pleased that you have been having fun while I keep myself pure for you, but maybe I am a little relieved too…'

He had never expected this reaction but, then, Luka remembered, she had always surprised him. Sophie had always made him either smile or want to tear his hair out in frustration. He'd never known what to expect from her.

'I thought—'

'You thought that I would cry and plead and say that you have shamed me. Well, I guess that in the eyes of everyone here you will have shamed me, but I don't care what they all think. I am nineteen tomorrow, Luka, and I want a life. I want more fun than I could have as your wife.'

'Were you ever going to tell me this?'

'I was.' Sophie smiled. 'But after we had made love. I went and got the Pill…'

'What, did you think I'd be more open to suggestion then?'

'That had crossed my mind.' She smiled again.

'You're really okay with it?' Luka frowned because this reaction had been far from the one he had been expecting.

'Of course,' she said, and then her voice dropped. 'Apart from one thing.'

Yes, she always surprised him.

'You still owe me that kiss.'

'Sophie, you don't end a relationship with a kiss.'

'Why not?' she said. 'I want you to be my first kiss.'

'Sophie—'

'It has to be you,' Sophie said, because quite simply it had to be. She sat on the kitchen bench and her hands went up and linked loosely behind his neck.

'Remember the party, the night you left for London?'

'Of course I remember.'

'Did you want to kiss me then?'

'No,' Luka said. Then she had been a girl, a teary teenager, now there was no doubt that a woman sat before him—and one who knew what she wanted.

'Do you want to kiss me now?' Sophie asked.

He answered with his lips. She felt the soft weight of his mouth and though she did not want to marry Luka, it did not mean she did not find him beautiful. Every kiss that Sophie had ever missed out on was made up for by this.

He held her face and his mouth was gentle. The last seconds of her lip glaze ensured their soft passage and his kiss was exactly as it should be, better even than anticipated. A soft tasting that had her hands move to his chest as they had ached to do on sight.

In her dreams he had crushed her mouth and his tongue had fiercely parted her lips, but in reality he had no need to for her mouth readily opened to his and mutually their kiss deepened.

Her palms pressed to his naked chest and as his tongue slipped in she slid her hands, loving the feeling of strength beneath the skin. His breathing was harsher as her hands moved over his flat, mahogany nipples and then it was Sophie who took his face in her hands.

She felt he was going to halt their kiss so her

tongue pleaded for him not to. She wanted this just as he did.

She wanted his hand that was now stroking at her breast through the fabric of her dress and as her nipple thickened to the touch of his thumb he let out a small moan that sent a vibration to her core. He stepped in closer and her legs parted to enable him to. One hand still toyed with her breast while the other slid up the outside of her smooth thigh, but when he encountered her naked bottom he stilled and pulled his mouth back a little.

'Do you always run around with no underwear on?'

'You'll never know.' Sophie smiled and Luka returned it but when she went to kiss him he moved his mouth back and she ached because he had halted. 'Please, Luka...'

'You said a kiss.'

'*We* want more than a kiss.'

She was so certain in that moment that she could speak for them both.

'I'm not ending things *and* taking your virginity,' Luka said. 'You've already got enough reasons to call me a bastard.'

'Then don't give me another one,' Sophie warned. 'I cried every night for a month when you left but I'm not going to cry this time. You've had all my tears, Luka. I just want a part of what was promised to me.'

'Which part?'

'This part.'

His eyes closed as her hand found him and she ran her fingers over his length. Lightly at first but then she pressed her fingers in a little.

She had never been shy around Luka.

She had never been shy.

She watched as he closed her eyes and felt the bliss as he grew to her touch. The ache in her groin grew too and so Sophie wriggled provocatively closer to the only man she had ever wanted.

She met his ear and kissed it as he pulled her in firmly.

'I want you to be my first.' She stated her wishes. 'It has to be you, Luka... It was *always* going to be you.'

CHAPTER FOUR

GONE WAS THE girl he had tipped from his knee all those years ago. Gone was the teary teenager. Instead of pleading, instead of crying, now she seduced.

Now she removed her hand from where it was teasing him and stopped the dance with her tongue on his ear so that she could watch his eyes open.

With a smile, in one lithe easy motion, she pulled off her dress and naked she sat before him, watching his eyes roam the lushness of her breasts.

'This part,' Sophie said again, and with her legs balanced on his hips she unzipped and freed him.

He was beautiful. His skin was soft and dark and together they watched her explore him till Luka could take it no more. He was there at her entrance and Sophie was guiding him in, her jaw tensing as he stretched her but the rest of her was loose and willing.

'Not here,' Luka said, even though it was contrary to his action, for he was inching just a little more inside her tight space.

'Yes, here,' Sophie urged.

They wanted each other's mouths yet the top of their heads were locked, watching as if from the edge of paradise as he inched in a little further. Bordo Del Cielo meant the edge of heaven and that was exactly where both of them were as he stretched her.

'Not here,' Luka warned again, despite her frantic pleas for him to continue. 'I'm taking you to my bed.'

He tried to zip up but with the protest of her kisses and the scent and oil of her on his fingers further turning him on it was like trying to reset a jack-in-the-box. He gave in and just kicked off his pants and got back to kissing her as he lifted her from the kitchen bench. With her legs coiled around him they kissed all the way up the stairs.

'Here,' Sophie said, when they were halfway up and he halted just to taste her deeper. He almost relented but then reminded himself of a part of the need for getting to his bedroom.

'I've got condoms in my case.'

'I told you we don't need them.'

They just made it to the bedroom and he dropped her onto the bed but, unlike the last time when he'd had had to peel her from him, now, loose-limbed, she let herself fall—because this time Sophie knew that in a moment he'd join her.

'I told you I've already gone on the Pill,' she said, watching the delicious sight of him kneeling and trying to open up his case.

'It's for protection.'

'I've never needed protection from you.'

Innocent, Luka thought, but only to a point. Her words were more seductive than any he had ever heard. Nothing would usually halt him—sheathing was, to Luka, second nature. Not with Sophie, though, because he wanted the naked bliss of them together. Later he would scold her, and warn her not to trust another with such a choice.

She was right, though; she needed no protection from him.

'I know what I want, Luka.'

He came over to the bed where she lay and like a panther he crawled with stealth that had her writhing until he was with her, and she would never forget his smile.

'I'm going to talk to you later.'

'You're going to make love to me now, though.' Sophie smiled back.

'Are you nervous?'

'I've never been nervous with you.'

It was true. Around him she was not nervous. How could she be scared? Sophie briefly pondered when the mouth that made her shiver returned to hers.

They kissed naked and long and then he left her mouth and blazed a hot, wet trail down her neck and then to her breasts, where he licked the warm skin, avoiding her aching nipples till her hands guided his head. It was Sophie who moaned as his mouth captured her and sucked deeply, not once, not twice, but over and over till she twitched and writhed. How could she be nervous when her body just came alive to him?

She loved how he gave the same attention to the other breast and yet she was almost pleading for him to stop because he had lifted just a fraction of the lid and she was greedy for the treasure he would bring.

Luka knew it.

He knelt up for a moment and looked down at her.

Her mouth was swollen from his kisses, her breasts were wet and her nipples erect, and there was a small purple bruise on her perfect skin that his mouth had made.

'Luka…' Sophie liked the warmth of his eyes and the affection of his gaze yet she was on fire. He was intimately stroking himself against her as he had downstairs, but there was no holding back as there had been then—this was just a moment of pure decadent indulgence.

She felt like his instrument, tuned purely for him to play to perfection, and he did. She looked down and this time watched him disappear further in.

'It might hurt,' Luka said.

'It had better.'

He laughed and toppled onto her. His weight was half on her and yet not enough; she liked the feeling of being lost beneath him—how the sight of the ocean from his window no longer existed, how the bark of a dog in the distance receded, how it was late in the afternoon and she welcomed the light just to see his closed eyes as he kissed her. Sophie's friends had needed wine, or long dances, some had demanded the promises of a love that would never die before this.

All Sophie needed was Luka, for this was just how it was supposed to be.

Luka was torn. He wanted to taste her breasts again, he wanted to kiss and make moist every inch of her skin, he wanted the musk of her sex on his tongue, not just his fingers. Badly he wanted her to come to his mouth, but he was as impatient to be inside as Sophie was to be taken.

Later, he told himself.

There would be time for that later.

Like a chip to his skull, somewhere he refuted that, because they ended today, this was it.

Yet there, in that second, Luka knew he would take her again, that this was not the end.

And, yes, he could feel her impatience. Her hips kept lifting, her mouth was more demanding and then there was almost anger as he removed his kiss.

'Luka.' She was breathless.

'Now!' Luka said, that one word taking such effort to deliver.

'Yes, now,' she said, but then she saw his slow, teasing smile.

'I mean *now* is when you can get anything you want from a man.' He was referring to her earlier innocent thinking. 'Not after...'

'I'll remember that for the future.'

She did not understand the flare of possession in his eyes as she spoke of others, but she didn't have time to dwell on it for he took her then. Luka seared into her and swallowed her sob with his mouth.

It hurt, far more than she had expected it to, far better than she had ever dared dream. He filled her and stretched her and, when she thought she knew what it was to be his lover, still further he went tearing at virgin flesh and then stilling as her body fought to acclimatise to him.

She forgot how to breathe until he gathered her right into him and hooked his arm beneath the small of her back.

'Luka...' Sophie didn't even know what she wanted or what it was she was trying to say, but as he started to move any pain was forgotten because with each thrust he made her more his. His mouth was by her ear now, and he spoke as he did in her dreams. 'I won't hurt you...' he said, when she now knew that he would.

The pain of being taken by him was receding. It was the pain of being left by him that was now starting to make itself known.

She wished that her body didn't love him so completely. She wished that he would take her deeper, harder, faster, rather than deliver, as he was now, the slow torture of his love, because that was exactly what this felt like.

As her legs coiled around him, even as she urged him on, Sophie was frantically trying to hold back.

How do I let you leave? she wanted to sob as her orgasm gathered.

'Luka...' She said it again as she started to come and the intensity scared her.

'Let it happen...' Luka said, and his rapid thrust gave her no choice but to do as his body commanded.

Inwardly he beat her to match his rhythm but it wasn't that that had her toppling over the edge, it was Luka, and the feel of his shoulders tense beneath her hands. It was the last look at the world without fully having the other, this strange brink they both found themselves on. Luka was in that beat before coming, past the point of no return when he felt her pulse to him and he just unleashed. Nothing could ever top this, he knew. Her intimate pulses beckoned and he gave in to the tight, soft warmth of her endless caress.

For Sophie it was the sensation of falling but not a gentle one.

Every bump, every sob, every fear seemed enacted in slow motion. She wanted to curl up in protection but his hands held down her arms. She hoped for a moment of clarity but he was pounding her senses again. Kissing her hard as his climax receded and then thrusting again, giving up the very last of himself as she lay there, knowing she had nothing left to give.

She had been taken.

CHAPTER FIVE

'SO THAT'S WHAT it feels like,' Sophie said.

'Not usually.'

They were lying in his bed and watching the evening sun over the ocean.

Sophie's head was resting on his chest and she watched a cruise liner glint in the distance.

'Not *usually*?' she checked.

'Truth?' he asked, and she nodded. 'There is usually a knot of disquiet.' He took her hand and he placed it just beneath where his ribs joined, and he pushed her fingers in. 'Just there.'

'Why?'

'I don't know,' he admitted.

He moved his hand to the same place on her. 'Do you have it?'

'No,' Sophie admitted. 'No knots, no disquiet.'

She knew what he meant, though, as she tried

to imagine a moment where the man lying there wasn't Luka.

It felt written in her DNA that this time belonged to him.

'You really want to work on them?' Luka asked, and they must have both been looking at the same thing because he voiced her thoughts.

'No, I really want to be a guest on one of them.' Sophie smiled. 'But for now working on one would be wonderful.'

'What would your father say?' Luka asked.

'What *will* my father say?' Sophie corrected, because it was going to happen, she was determined, but she answered his question. 'I don't know how he's going to react,' she said, listening to the thud of Luka's heart as he stroked her hair. So much had changed now. 'I guess people will understand that I might want to get away after the shame of you dumping me.' She laughed and dug him in the ribs but then she was serious. 'I don't know how my father will be about it but I don't think I can factor that in when I make my choice… I don't know if I want to stay here in Bordo Del Cielo, Luka. There is too much past…'

They were the same, Luka realised.

'I think my father is up to no good,' Sophie admitted. 'I love him yet I want to get away from him. I want no part in that type of life.'

During his last years at school Luka had started to question the way things worked here and he had fought hard to go to university in England. There, his eyes had been fully opened as to his father's ways and from that distance he had decided to stay away.

Sophie had worked it out from here, Luka thought.

Or was starting to.

'My father doesn't work, he sits in a bar most of the day and into the night. What are these meetings he says that he has to go to?' She looked up from his chest and instead of giving her an answer or avoiding the subject he offered the unexpected.

'Come to London with me,' Luka said.

'With you?'

'You could apply to the cruise liners from there. I could help you to get on your feet. I am a part owner of a hotel, you could work there till you get your dream job...'

Sophie lay there, thinking about it. She wasn't surprised that he part owned a hotel—Malvolio would have seen to it that his son was looked after.

'I have a flat,' Luka said. 'You could stay with me for a while.'

'Stay with you?' Sophie blinked. 'I don't know if that would work out...'

'Why not?'

'Luka, while I accept this is a one-off, I really don't want to be there if you bring another woman home...'

It angered her that he laughed and Sophie climbed from the bed. 'I'm going to have a shower and then I have to go to church...' She stopped talking when she saw the sheets that bore the evidence of what had just taken place. 'Oh.'

'I'll sort it all out,' Luka said. 'I'm not going

to leave them for Angela. Go and have your shower...'

As Sophie did so she thought about what Luka had suggested and she thought too about her cross response.

It was true.

She somehow had to hold in her jealousy at the thought of him with someone else. She'd agreed to break things off, a part of her had even been happy about it and certainly she had been relieved...

That had been before they'd made love, though.

How could once with Luka ever be enough?

He had taken her, left her exhausted and sated.

Now, though, even the recent memory was bringing her back to sensual life. She soaped her tender breasts and saw the bruise that his mouth had made. Her sex was hot and swollen and as Sophie soaped the last traces of him away she wanted him again.

She walked out with a towel around her to the sight of a naked Luka changing the sheets. Now from a relative distance she could admire his naked beauty. He was tall and lean and she could see the muscles on his thighs as he bent to rather haphazardly tuck in the sheet. His shaft, though soft against his leg, lifted a little from the movement and she wanted to take the sheet from his hand and get back to bed.

'Is that the first bed you have ever made?' Sophie teased, trying to keep things light.

'It is the first bed I have ever made in Bordo Del Cielo,' Luka answered. He looked to where she stood and wondered if what he had to offer would be enough. She thought him rich and, in London, he wasn't.

Yet.

'Sophie, I have a small flat in London...' Luka would explain it all to her later, he decided. He would go into detail about how he had removed himself completely from his father, that his ways were honest. But he wasn't going to do that here, and anyway there was something else that needed to be addressed before they got to family stuff. Today was about them, about the possibility of a future away from Bordo Del Cielo. 'What you said before about me bringing another woman home if we lived in London, I would not do that to you. In the same way I wouldn't like it if you were staying with me and saw anyone else...'

'I don't understand what you are saying.'

'I'm saying that I don't want it to be over between us. Maybe I don't want to commit to marriage, or getting engaged just yet, it is far too soon for that, but we can date,' Luka said. 'Once we get to London we can go out and get to know each other away from our families. We can do things our way, without all the pressure and expectations.'

Sophie could feel the goose-bumps on her bare arms as she realised that Luka wasn't just offering her a way out of Bordo Del Cielio but a way out *with* him.

'Can I still apply to work on the cruise liners if we are going out with each other?'

'Sophie,' Luka said. 'Tomorrow you are nineteen, of course you must follow your dreams and do the work you want to.' He threw a sheet at her. 'For now, though, you can help me do this...'

Sophie took the sheet and started making her side of the bed. 'Does anything smell better than a sheet dried in the sun?' Sophie asked, because at the hotel it was all starch and bleach.

'One thing does,' Luka said, and he beckoned her to cross the bed. Unabashed, wanting the same as him, she climbed over to him, kneeling up as he stood. 'You do.'

'And you,' Sophie said.

They kissed a slow, long kiss that she wanted to go on for ever but it was Luka who halted things—the sky was turning orange, he could hear the bell in the distance, summoning everyone to church. He had no intention of going himself but he knew that Sophie would be expected to be there so he pulled back. 'I'll go and get your dress. You said you needed to be at church.'

'Soon,' Sophie said.

'You'll be late,' Luka said.

'I'm always late.'

'When we're in London, we can spend the whole day…' He didn't finish. Her towel was slipping and Sophie let it fall. His lovely erection was nudging her stomach as they kissed some more.

'I want to kiss you there,' Sophie said, and now, when she lowered her head, Luka didn't remind her that there was somewhere else she needed to be.

She kissed down his stomach until his erection was too tempting at her cheek to ignore. He held the base as she tasted him first with her tongue then kissed him along his thick shaft and then Luka removed his hands.

Sophie felt giddy as she ran her lips over the salty tip.

Together they would go to London; they would get to know each other's bodies.

The world was theirs.

'Like this?' Sophie asked, and then parted her lips and took him a little way in.

'Like that,' Luka agreed. This, for Luka, was more intimate than sex. More private. He would prefer to give rather than take but he went with it now. His hands were in her hair and she felt the building pressure. 'Deeper,' Luka said, and she obliged, taking him in as far as she could as her tongue swirled on his shaft.

His powerful thighs started to buck a little, his hand coiled her hair into a long ponytail and Sophie loved the traction—the tightness to her scalp gave her delicious direction but then cruelly she stopped.

'Now?' Sophie said, hovering over him, and then she looked up and smiled as he swore. 'Is now a good time to get my own way?'

'Why the hell did I tell you that?' Luka both laughed and groaned. 'What is it that you want?'

'Can Bella come too?' Sophie asked. 'Just till we get on our feet?'

'Sophie...' Luka tried to come up with a reason why she couldn't but, what he hell, he knew Bella and Sophie had been friends for ever and it might make it easier for Sophie to settle in. 'Sure,' Luka said. 'Bella can come too. Now, get back to work.'

Laughing, happy, she did so. Her hands moved and held his taut buttocks. He let her hair fall and what went on behind the black curtain was a private tasting. Sophie rested on her heels, her sex on fire as Luka didn't try for gentle. She loved his passion, how he told her exactly what he wanted—which was simply more of the same. It was hot work and then he swore again, and it was right to swear because things could never be the same as he swelled in her throat, she pulled her head back and caught him first on her tongue, tasting and swallowing him down, more turned on than she thought possible. But then she realised he hadn't finished, and the sound of him gently swearing as he came over her lips and into her hair had her close to climax.

'Tonight...' Luka scooped her up to him, told her he would wash himself out of her hair, right now in the shower, and then, 'I shall go and speak to your father tonight.'

Not yet, though. He saw her so flushed and aroused and ready that he pushed her back on the bed. Too giddy to stand, he knelt on the floor. She would take a minute. Luka knew. She was almost there. He could see her wet, sore and swollen, her clitoris erect, and God help him but he never wanted them to get out of bed.

Sophie watched, shocked and laughing, as he pulled her to his mouth, and she lay there longing for the building pressure in her to release to his lips. She would later wish she could somehow hold that moment, for it was a time that belonged only to them. A time of pure happiness. A moment without shame, where the future was bright, where dreams were coming true, but then a crashing noise doused her in panic.

There was the sound of footsteps running up the stairs.

A lot of them.

Her first thought was that Malvolio had come home, though there was too much noise for it to be only him, but then the police shouted out that they were being raided.

Luka threw a sheet over her. The bedroom door splintered and as it was kicked open he lay over her as gruff voices told them not to move.

'Non muovetevi!'

Sophie closed her eyes in terror as Luka was hauled from the bed to the floor where he was cuffed.

'Stay still,' Luka warned her. 'Just stay calm.' Then he shouted to them to fetch her clothes but all they gave her was one of Luka's shirts.

'Not in church this evening?' The lewd comment only added to her embarrassment and terror as Sophie attempted to cover herself.

'Say nothing,' Luka warned her. His voice was the only calm in the room but then it changed as they pulled Sophie's hands behind her back and put on cuffs. 'Why are you cuffing her?'

'I don't know what's happening...' Sophie said, and then she looked at Luka, met his eyes and in that moment she did know.

This was about their fathers.

'Say nothing,' Luka said. 'I'll get you a lawyer.'

It had all been perfect and now she had been plunged into a hell that burned ever hotter. Sophie was unceremoniously marched to a car. The entire congregation of the church, it seemed, had come out and were watching from the other side of the road. It was mortifying. The only saving grace was Bella, shouting to her friend, 'I'll get some clothes and bring them.' She was already running down the hill towards Sophie's home.

There was no time to thank Bella. Instead, Sophie's head was pushed down as she got into a police car, but it didn't come close to the loving way Luka's hand had, only moments ago, guided her head.

'*Poutana...*' She heard the whispers—some even said it loudly. The people she had grown up with had all turned on her in one night and very soon she would start to understand why.

'I suggest you *don't* take your boyfriend's advice and that you do speak,' Sophie was told as the car started to drive off

Sophie said nothing. She trusted Luka to sort this out and she knew that she'd done nothing wrong. She rested her head against the window and lifted her hands to her tousled hair, feeling her mother's earring, then moved her fingers to her other ear.

It was gone.

'My earring,' she started, and then stopped. She would speak with Luka later. It had to be in his bedroom, or maybe on the path as she had been led out.

She looked down at the car floor, wondering if she had lost it when she'd been pushed in.

'So where's your father tonight?' she was asked, but Sophie refused to answer. She had given up looking for her earring and was now back to staring unseeingly out of the window,

'There's Luka's father,' the officer said, and Sophie started to breathe faster as she saw Malvolio being led by the police from the hotel. 'I wonder where Paulo is,' the policeman said. 'Let's take the scenic route.' But instead of the beach road they were heading now towards the hotel and into a small side street, the same street that Sophie had walked down just a few hours ago. Now, though, it was filled with firefighters and the deli was alight with flames.

'You were in there this afternoon, weren't you?' the officer checked, and there was no point denying it so Sophie nodded.

'Your father went and visited them this morning,' the officer said. 'For the third time.'

It was then, Sophie knew, time for her to start talking.

CHAPTER SIX

'SOPHIE DURANTE.'

Sophie stood as her name was called.

It had taken six long months to get to the trial.

After the arrests she had been released without charge the next morning but her father, Luka and Malvolio had all been charged with various offences.

The last six months she had spent living with Bella and her mother because, even from prison, Malvolio still ruled Bordo Del Cielo. Her father's house had been signed over to him to pay for Paulo's lawyer.

Sophie had been allowed a few short, monitored visits with her father.

She would have preferred to have seen Luka.

It was a terrible thing to admit perhaps, but at every visit she had ached for just a glimpse of him and she could no longer look her father in the eye.

'You will hear many things in the trial,' Paulo had said. 'Some of the things will be true, but most are lies...'

Sophie simply didn't know what to believe.

Trinkets and jewellery had been found in their home. Souvenirs, the police called them, for they had all belonged to victims.

Sophie knew they had not been in her home, she'd cleaned it after all. But she also knew that her father, though perhaps not a killer, had not been entirely innocent either and it hurt like hell to know that.

'Malvolio would send me to warn people—it doesn't mean that I hurt them...' Paulo attempted to explain.

'You went, though,' Sophie shot back. 'You terrified them just by passing on the warnings. Why would you say yes to him?'

'Sophie, please—'

'No!' She would not simply ignore the facts.

'You chose to say yes to him and, please, never say that you did it for me. He kept us poor.'

'You have Luka.'

Sophie let out an incredulous laugh. 'Don't tell me you said yes to him just for that. I'd have had Luka with or without your help.'

She was confident of that.

Almost.

She couldn't wait for the trial to be over, to go with him to London...to take up those tentative dreams and to run with them.

Sophie looked at her father. He looked so grey and gaunt and she knew she had to win the battle to forgive him and stand by him, for she was the only family that he had.

'After the trial you can get away from Bordo Del Cielo and start over again,' Sophie said.

'I'm not leaving your mother.'

'She's been dead for seventeen years! Father, I am going to be leaving. I'm going to move to London with Luka. I just want to get away from here and all the people who have judged me.' She ran a nervous tongue over her lips for there was

one thing she felt her father ought to hear first
from her. 'You will hear things in court about
me too, father. Things that you won't like. That
afternoon, when the raids happened, Luka and
I...we were together.'

'Sophie, you and Luka were practically engaged. You have nothing to be ashamed about.
Walk into that court and give your evidence with
your head held high.'

How, though?

As her father was led back to the cells Sophie
asked, as she always did, if she could visit Luka.

He had no one. His mother had died years ago
and his father was locked away.

'Non ci sono visitatori ammessi.'

Again she was told that no visitors were allowed and then she found out that Luka had been
placed in solitary.

'Malvolio too?' Sophie challenged. 'Of course
not.' She answered her own question.

Luka wasn't a security risk, Luka wouldn't con-
taminate the trial, that would be Malvolio.

'He rules even in here,' Sophie called out as she left on the eve of the trial.

She took the bus back to Bordo Del Cielo and walked down the street.

Teresa's café was all boarded up and the locals shunned her. If it weren't for Bella and her mother. she would have had nowhere to go.

If it weren't for Luka, she wouldn't even be here, a still small voice told her.

She was so cross with her father that there was a temptation to simply take the next flight and leave him to his fate, given all he had done.

But Luka…

He was the reason she was here.

Sophie halted at Giovanni's the jewellers when she saw him at the window, adding a new stand to the wares. 'Anything?' she asked when he caught her eye, because she was still hoping against hope that her earring might have been found and handed in.

Giovanni shook his head and disappeared back into the shop, leaving Sophie standing there.

No one wanted to be seen talking with her.

She peered in and looked at the new offerings in the window. There was a huge emerald-cut diamond set on the prettiest rose gold band and she couldn't help but let her imagination take flight.

She wanted that ring on her finger.

Or rather she wanted the engagement that had never taken place.

Walking back to Bella's, she tasted the salty sea air and thought of Luka alone and locked away.

He had no one.

Well, he did, he had her, but there was no way to let him know, apart from to do as her father said and to walk into the trial with her head held high. She would not be ashamed about what had taken place between her and Luka that afternoon.

She was here only for him.

Sophie tried.

Throughout the trial, as a witness she had not been admitted to the courtroom, but today she was being called to give evidence and, though dreading it, though embarrassed at the thought of some of the salacious details of that day being examined, though scared for her father, what had sustained her was that today she would see Luka.

And she did.

Walking into the courtroom to take the stand, finally she saw him. Those navy eyes met hers and he gave her a small encouraging smile. He looked thinner, leaner and sharper. The scar above his eye had had little medical attention for it had healed badly and even from the witness stand she could see it purple and raised. His hair was cut far too short and Sophie could see the anger that simmered beneath the surface, though not towards her, for his eyes were kind when they met hers.

She awaited the barrage of questions and let out a breath of relief when the rather embarrassing moments of the police raid were skimmed over.

'You knew that Teresa was upset with you that day when you went into the deli?'

'I did?'

'And you asked your father why she might be upset?'

'I just mentioned it in passing when I got home.' Sophie swallowed, her cheeks going a little bit pink as they made it sound as if she had been questioning her father. 'I thought it was to do with my upcoming engagement, that because Malvolio would be my father-in-law...'

'Just answer the question.'

Sophie frowned, as she did on many occasions over a very long day of questioning. Malvolio and Luka had the same lawyer, her father had a different one, yet even he wasn't asking the pertinent questions.

'The souvenirs that the police say they found in my home...' Sophie attempted, for when she had been arrested, over and over the police had spoken about trinkets that had belonged to the deceased or come from buildings that had been destroyed. She wanted to explain they had never been in her home. That she had kept the house and would have known if such things were there.

'We'll get to that later,' her father's lawyer said, yet he did not.

Sophie left the witness stand and now that she had given her evidence she was allowed to watch as the accused were cross-examined.

Malvolio went to the witness stand a sinner but the questions were so gentle and so geared for him that he left the stand looking like a saint and walked away with an arrogant smile.

She sat bewildered as her father took the stand. He seemed weak and confused. Sophie once stood and shouted as his own lawyer misled him but Bella pulled her down.

'Quiet, or you will be asked to leave.'

'It's not fair, though,' Sophie said.

None of it was fair.

Yes, her father admitted, a second visit from him meant there would be trouble if bills were not paid.

A third visit was the final warning.

'I had no choice but to do as Malvolio said.'

It was, Sophie knew, a poor defence.

And then it was Luka.

In a dark suit and tie, his skin was pale from months of being locked inside. He wrenched his arm from a guard who led him, still as defiant, still as silent as he had been on the day of his arrest.

He would not lie to save his father.

Luka refused to lie.

It was not in him to lie and he wanted no part of his father's life so he had decided that he would speak the truth.

The truth could not hurt him.

Or so he thought.

He looked out and nodded to his close friend Matteo, who had been there every day to support him, and then he looked at Sophie. He tried to let her know with his eyes that he had this under control.

But ten minutes into his testimony he started to glimpse his father's game.

'Did your concerns about Paulo's dealings play any part in your decision to not go ahead with your engagement to his daughter Sophie Durante?'

There was a gasp around the courtroom and Sophie stared ahead as Bella took her hand.

'Sophie and I had decided to make our own arrangements for the future,' Luka answered in a clear voice.

'We'll get back to that but first can you answer the question? Did you have concerns about Paulo's dealings?'

'I had never really given Paulo much thought,' Luka answered, though his voice was not quite so clear as he delivered his response.

'Did Sophie tell you that she had concerns about her father's activities?'

His already pale face bleached and he looked into Sophie's eyes briefly. He had sworn to tell the truth but he could not have Sophie's own words be the reason for Paulo being put away.

'No, she did not.' For her, Luka lied under oath.

'So what you did discuss that day?'

'I really can't remember,' Luka answered.

'Because you were busy in the bedroom?' His lawyer was working more for Malvolio, Luka knew it now. Luka didn't have anything to hide so the lawyer would work to secure his father's freedom by throwing Paulo under the bus.

'I'm confused,' the lawyer continued. 'On the afternoon in question you said to your father that you were going to end things with Sophie, yes?'

'Yes,' Luka answered. 'However—'

'Malvolio was upset,' the lawyer broke in. 'In fact, you got into a fight when you spoke poorly about the woman he had chosen with care for you. You said that you did not want to marry a peasant of his choice. Correct?'

Sophie closed her eyes and then forced them open as Luka was forced to admit that, yes, that had been what he had said.

'I was trying to separate myself from my father—' He didn't get to finish.

'You told your father that you preferred the more glamorous, sophisticated women in London to Sophie. Now do you see the reason for my confusion? Sophie Durante came to your home...'

'My father sent for Sophie so that he could move the souvenirs to Paulo's,' Luka said. He could see what had happened now. Six months locked up, two of them spent in solitary, had given him a lot of time to think. His father hadn't been hoping to get Sophie and him together, Luka was sure of that now. Malvolio must have been tipped off about the raids and would have wanted the souvenirs out of his home and in Paulo's.

Only no one wanted to hear his truth.

'Sophie Durante heard that you were about to renege on your promise to marry her. She turned up at your home on a Sunday afternoon to dissuade you and you ended up in bed that same afternoon, or rather you had sex in the kitchen.'

'No.'

'You are saying nothing happened in the kitchen?' the lawyer checked.

'As I have said, I had had a fight with my father, Sophie was sorting out the cut above my eye...'

'Oh, I see—you were bleeding so profusely that she was left with no choice but to take off her dress to stem the bleed...?' the lawyer asked, and Sophie sat burning with shame, completely humiliated as the courtroom laughed.

'My father had suggested that Sophie come over before I told him that I did not want to get engaged. He wanted her out of Paulo's house so that he could move—'

'Did Sophie Durante want to be out of that house too?' the lawyer interrupted. 'Was Sophie concerned that her father was engaged in criminal activity? Did she tell you she wanted to get away from him?'

Luka broke into a cold sweat, he could feel it trickle down his back. He was doing everything he could to stay calm, to somehow give his version of events, but there was no right answer.

His father had a brilliant lawyer, so too did he, and he was, Luka could now see, being used to discredit Paulo.

If he answered yes to the question then he put Paulo away for life.

'No.'

'You are under oath,' the lawyer reminded him.

'No, she did not say that.' Luka's voice was clear as he decided that bedroom talk had no place in the courtroom.

'You did tell your father, though, that you were not going to go ahead with the engagement?'

'Yes.'

'And you told Sophie the same. Yes or no?'

'Yes.'

'Luka.' The lawyer really was the smiling assassin as he looked at his youngest client, whose father was paying the hefty bill. 'How can you expect the court to believe that there was no conversation—?'

'We were *otherwise* engaged.'

'*After* you had ended things?'

'Yes.'

'Nothing was said about her father?'

Luka did what he had to.

'There really was little conversation.'

'It makes no sense.'

The lawyer was about to pounce again but Luka got there first and turned to the judge and shrugged his shoulders. 'I think that Sophie might have been trying to get me to change my mind about ending things by trying to seduce me so I took what was on offer.' He looked out towards the jury and then back to the judge as he shamed her. 'Am I on trial for my libido?'

The laughter that went around the courtroom ended the testimony.

But as Luka left the stand she did not look at him.

Luka knew that he might have saved her father from conviction by his own daughter's words.

But it might just have killed the two of them.

CHAPTER SEVEN

SOPHIE, EVEN DAYS LATER, could not bring herself to look at Luka as the defendants stood to hear their fate.

'He didn't mean it.' Over and over Bella said this to Sophie, who had held in her formidable temper since Luka had said those words. 'The lawyer gave him no choice.'

The villagers sniggered as she passed, there were whispers everywhere she went, but now, as the verdict was about to be delivered, there were no smiles or laughter in court.

All knew that the six-month break they'd had from Malvolio's clutches might end today.

'Luka Romano Cavaliere—*non colpevole.*'

Despite her anger, Sophie let out a breath of relief and she did lift her eyes to look at him. She didn't expect his eyes to be waiting for hers, yet they were. For a small slice of time they stared at the other and the courtroom faded.

He gave her a nod that apologised, that said he would explain things, that soon he would be with her.

'Here comes the verdict for Malvolio,' Bella whispered.

'Malvolio Cavaliere—*non colpevole.*'

'No!' Bella gasped, and Sophie clutched her friend's hand as the fat brute smiled over in their direction.

Malvolio had wanted Bella for a long time.

Pandemonium broke out as, terrified now and determined to appear loyal to Malvolio, the spectators in the courtroom applauded. Sophie simply lowered her head and tried not to weep.

She knew what was coming.

Her father was so frail he could hardly stand.

Paulo Durante—*colpevole.*

Her father would be taken to the mainland for sentencing, the court was informed, and would serve out his time there.

He would die in prison, Sophie knew that.

She watched him being led away and though she was still angry at him she knew she was the only person that he had so she called out to him, 'I'll be there for you...'

She would be.

There were cheers in the streets as Malvolio left the court a free man, though Sophie didn't hear them and neither did she wait to speak with Luka; instead, she went to Bella's to start packing.

'I'm going to Rome to be near him and you need to leave too,' Sophie urged Bella. 'Malvolio is back, all his yes-men are still here.'

'I cannot leave my mother,' Bella said .

'She will understand...'

'I can't, Sophie, she is so sick.'

There was a knock on the door and Bella went to answer it as Sophie continued to pack.

'No,' Sophie said as Bella returned. 'I don't want to see him.'

'It wasn't Luka,' Bella said, and Sophie looked up when she heard the strain in her friend's voice. 'It was Pino with a message for me. There is to be a big celebration tonight at the hotel, everyone is to be there. I am to work in the bar.'

'No!' Sophie was adamant. 'You are to come with me to Roma.'

'I can't leave her now,' Bella said. 'I know that you have to leave and not just to take care of Paulo—you are the scapegoat now. Everyone knows it is Malvolio but that is not what that will say to his face.' Bella started to cry. 'I don't want my first to be Malvolio. I know you think I should just say no to him.'

'I know that it is not that simple.' Sophie put her arm around her friend, who took a cleansing breath.

'When my mother has gone, and it won't be long, I will come to Rome and be with you. But not now. I need to be here for her in the same way you need to be there for your father.'

There was a knock at the door and Bella went to answer it and after a moment came back and this time, Bella told Sophie, it was Luka here to see her.

'I have nothing to say to him.'

'He says he's not leaving till he has spoken with you.'

He wouldn't leave, Sophie knew it.

Her shame and hurt from the words he had said in court the other day was still there inside her. Her fear, her panic about her father seemed to be swirling into a concentrated storm as finally, for the first time in six months, they would speak.

She stepped out of the small bedroom and there Luka stood in the hall. 'Congratulations,' she hurled at him. 'You and your father walk free, while mine is to be imprisoned on the mainland. Where is the justice?'

'There is no justice,' Luka said. 'Can we go for a walk?'

'Just say what you have to.'

'Not here,' Luka said, and looked over to the bedroom that Bella was in.

'I trust Bella,' Sophie said, 'And, given all that was said, I trust her far more than I trust you.'

'You know why I had to say what I did.'

Somewhere deep down Sophie did. Right there, in the midst of her turmoil, she did know that so she nodded and called to Bella that she was heading out for a short while.

They walked from Bella's home down the street and past the hotel Brezza Oceana, not talking at first. Cars were starting to arrive, there were flowers being brought in through the foyer. Clearly the hotel was preparing for a large celebration.

And, Sophie knew, Bella would be working there tonight and every other night that Malvolio dictated.

Yes, her heart hurt right now.

'Will you be going to the celebration tonight?' Sophie broke the strained silence.

'No,' Luka answered. 'I am having nothing more to do with my father.' They walked further on and they came to the small path that only the locals knew about and they walked down to the cove.

It felt strange being here with Luka when usually she came with Bella, and she told him that. 'We always called it our secret cove. I guess everyone does that, though.' She tried to make small talk but found it impossible, the hurt was too great.

Luka didn't even try.

'Sophie, tomorrow I am leaving for London. I want you to come with me and Bella too. Matteo is also leaving, though no one knows that yet. He will go along with things tonight and make out that he is pleased to see my father released but tomorrow he's getting out.'

'Bella can't leave her mother,'

'Bella has to,' Luka said.

'She won't. I just spoke to her and she says that she can't leave and I understand why. Her mother needs Bella to be working to pay the rent. She used to own her own home till *your* father took it from them to *help* cover the medical bills.'

Luka knew that, he knew it all now, but hearing the slight acid in Sophie's words that inferred his father's dealing were somehow anything to do with him had anger building within him, yet he fought to stay calm.

'I have to support her choice,' Sophie said.

They kept on walking and it was strange that

a place could be so picture perfect and yet so sordid.

'Sophie, will you come with me to London?'

'No,' Sophie said. 'I need to be close to my father. I'm going to go Rome and live there.'

'If you come to London with me then I can pay for you to visit him frequently.'

'I don't want you paying for me,' Sophie said. 'God, you're as arrogant as your father. Well, let me tell you—I would rather work as a *poutana* in the bar with Bella than go to London with you. Have you any idea of the shame, to stand the court and hear that?'

'Sophie.' He grabbed her arm and swung her around to face him. 'You know why I said what I did. I did all I could so that what you said to me would have no bearing on your father's verdict.'

But she didn't want to hear it.

'Go and live in London, Luka, and party with your models, who only want you for looks and money. You'll suit each other. Take the head start your father's filthy dealings gave you.'

'He gave me nothing.'

'Please,' Sophie scoffed. 'I'll do better on my own that I ever could with you.'

'Are you sure about that?' Luka checked.

'More than sure.'

'Some welcome,' Luka sneered, and then shook his head. 'I've been in prison for six months, two of them spent in solitary, where the thought of seeing you was the only thing that kept me sane.'

Luka had had a lot of time to think and in that time the only thing that had kept him going had been her and the memory of that afternoon—sheets that had smelt like the sun and the future they had dared to glimpse. He had walked out of court and straight to the jeweller's. It had been closed, of course, but he had gone around to Giovanni's home and asked him to open up, and his first purchase had been the thing he craved most.

A future with the person he loved by his side.

'What exactly did you say to your father?' Sophie demanded. 'I want to hear it.'

Now, instead of looking to the future, Sophie wanted to examine the past.

'I've just been found not guilty, Sophie. I've just had my past and my all my dealings examined. I never thought I'd have to come out to be to be retried by you. I lied under oath for you.'

'I don't care about your lies under oath,' Sophie said, her eyes blazing with anger. 'I care about the parts that were true. You go to London, Luka, you go with your glamorous women, you don't need to take the *peasant* along...'

It was that part that had killed her, that part that made her want to curl up right now and hide for ever, but instead Sophie came out fighting. She had never felt good enough for Luka, and hearing what he had said about her to his father had been more shameful than being paraded half-naked in front of the village. 'You weren't lying under oath then, Luka.'

'It was a row that I had with my father. What I said was wrong, I know that. Sophie, I thought it the moment I opened the door to you and saw you standing there, so beautiful...'

Unwittingly he had hurt her again. The Sophie he had seen that day had been dressed in her finest, but he couldn't know that. All his words did were reinforce her silent fear that if he knew the real Sophie, she wouldn't be good enough.

From the ruins she had to dig deep to find her pride.

'I'll never forgive you for that,' Sophie spat. 'I'll never forget the shame of my first lover calling me a peasant.'

'Well, it was it clearly true.' He hit completely below the belt but, hell, he was hurting. 'Do you really think I want to be standing arguing, with you acting like a fishwife, on the night I get set free? I want champagne, Sophie. I want laughter and a beautiful woman.'

'And?' she demanded.

'That about does it for me,' Luka said, and shrugged her off.

CHAPTER EIGHT

HE DIDN'T FEEL ANYTHING.

Or rather, Luka thought as the car took him from the airport to Bordo Del Cielo , the feelings that he had were perhaps not at they should be on the day of his father's funeral.

Yes, he was grieving.

Just not for Malvolio.

It had been five years since Luka had been back.

At least physically.

More than Luka cared to admit, his dreams regularly brought him back to this place.

The car turned and he looked out at the glittering Mediterranean and then another turn and there spread out before him were his childhood and teenage years.

The church, the houses, the rivers and roads

that were all etched in his heart were on view now. Memories of summers and Christmases long gone when he had lived a life with the promise of Sophie in his future.

It had been a promise that he had backed out on, Luka reminded himself.

Today, on the day that his father was buried, when surely there should be a layer of grief for his father, instead it was all for Sophie and for that small slice of time they had been together.

She still resided in his heart.

With the benefit of hindsight he had often rearranged that day in his mind so that they had left for London as soon as she had come out of the shower, before the raid, before everything had fallen apart.

He arrived at the church and as he stepped inside Luka could only give a wry smile for it was practically empty.

Defiant only on Malvolio's death, no one attended.

There was just Angela the maid, sitting midway down the aisle, and Luka gave her a nod and then headed to the front.

There was the sound of the door opening and he turned around because, yes, hope remained.

False hope, Luka thought as Pino, once a young boy on his bike, now a young man, came in and took a seat.

Luka nodded to him also but as he sat through the short service still his mind turned to Sophie.

She should have been here.

Had she cared for him, she would have been beside him today.

The burial was a sad joke.

Malvolio had paid for his own funeral and the huge oak casket with its glitzy trimmings went almost unnoticed, for everyone had chosen to stay at home.

Pino headed off and after Luka had thanked the priest he walked out of the cemetery with Angela.

'I have put on some refreshments,' Angela said, 'back at the house. I wasn't sure how many would be attending. I don't think I'll be hungry for a long time.'

Luka gave a wry smile. 'You know, for all his power and wealth he had nothing,' he said. 'Nothing that matters anyway.'

'I thought Matteo might come with you today. I hear that the two of you are doing very well.'

'He is in the Middle East on business. He offered to come but I really just wanted to do this on my own.'

Or not on his own. Still his eyes scanned the street, hoping against hope that she might yet arrive.

He should leave now.

Luka knew that.

His lawyers were taking care of the estate. Luka could barely stand to hear the details—his father owned Paulo's home and Bella's mother's too.

That was the mere start.

Most of the town had been handed over to his father in times of weakness or ill health, with the promise that Malvolio would take care of everything.

No wonder the church had been practically

empty. No doubt the moment Luka left they would celebrate the end of his father's dictatorship.

They would, Luka knew, have reason to celebrate properly soon for he had instructed his lawyers carefully.

He needed nothing from his father's estate. It would take some work and a lot of unravelling but, in time, all the homes that his father had procured through less than honourable means would be returned to their rightful owners or their descendants. The locals would only find that out long after he had left Bordo Del Cielo, though.

They arrived at his car and Luka looked at Angela's tired, strained face.

'How long until I have to leave the house?' Angela asked.

'You don't ever have to leave,' Luka said. Yes, he was handing it over to his lawyers, but he did not want Angela spending another night in fear. 'I will be transferring the house into your name.'

'Luka!' Angela shook her head. 'Bordo Del

Cielo is a popular holiday resort now, the properties are expensive.'

'It is your home,' Luka said. 'Hopefully, now it can be a happier one.' He gave her a small smile. 'Can I ask you to keep it to yourself for a little while?'

Angela nodded tearfully.

'Come back to the house,' she said, but Luka shook his head.

'There are few good memories there...'

'Come back for a little while at least.'

There was one good memory, though, and after a moment of quiet thought Luka nodded.

He hadn't been home since the night of the police raid.

On his release, after pleading with Sophie to join him in London, instead of going to the bar to celebrate his and his father's freedom he had sat on the sand, going over and over Sophie's words.

He went over them again now as he stepped into the kitchen and remembered her sitting on the bench and tending to his eye.

'I might take a look around,' Luka said, and

took the stairs, trying and failing not to remember their frantic kisses there, and then went into his old bedroom.

It was like entering a time warp.

Angela must have dusted it but it was just as he had left it.

Luka closed his eyes as he remembered that afternoon before it had all gone so wrong.

He thought of the plans they had made and their hopes for the future. Now, with the wisdom the years had afforded and after so many fleeting relationships that never came close to what he had found with Sophie, he knew that what had been born that day had been a fledgling love. It had to have been for there had been nothing close to the same since. Not just the sex, but the conversation, the sharing, peering into the future with one another and picturing themselves there—not clearly, they'd had but a few hours together, of course, but there had been the chance of a future and it had been stolen from them that same day.

He opened up his bedside drawer, expecting nothing, an old notebook perhaps or a school report. He used to hide them from his father—they had never been good enough. What he found, though, made him sit on the bed with his head in his hands.

Her earring—just a thin gold loop with a small diamond where the clasp met, but it was the only tangible thing he had from that day and he examined it carefully as memories rushed in. He remembered her standing at the door and how that tiny stone and the sparkle it had made had brought attention not to the earring but to her eyes.

She should have been here today, standing beside him. If she cared at all she'd have made the effort, wouldn't she?

'Did you ever look her up?' Angela asked a little later as they drank coffee.

'Who?' Luka attempted.

'The woman you were promised to for half of your life,' Angela said. 'The woman who walked out of this house dressed only in your shirt as the whole town looked on. The woman you shamed in court. I'm sure you don't need me to tell you her name.'

'I had no choice to say what I did in court.'

'I know that.'

'Sophie didn't, though.'

'She was young,' Angela said, and Luka nodded.

'She was more upset about what I said to my father about her being a peasant...' Luka smiled as he rolled his eyes. 'And so, to make things worse, I went and said it again on the beach, the night of my release...'

'To Sophie!' Angela exclaimed, but then smiled. 'She is so like her mother. Rosa could skin you alive with her eyes...I remember the day she turned up here, shouting at Malvolio to leave her family alone...' Her voice trailed off. Even if he was dead, some things still weren't discussed, but Luka nodded.

He could remember that day just a little. Rosa had knocked on the door and had stood shouting down the hallway.

He'd forgotten that, Luka thought. He would have been eight or nine…

'You were younger then too when you said those things and you were also just out of prison.' Angela broke into his thoughts. 'Perhaps it wasn't the time for common sense.'

Again, he nodded.

'So, *did* you ever look her up?'

'I sat in a car outside Paulo's jail day in day out for a month a couple of years ago,' Luka admitted. 'Then I found out that he was in hospital and not even there.'

'You never visited him?'

'I couldn't face him,' Luka admitted. 'He took the fall for my father. When I found out that he had been sentenced to forty-three years…' Luka gave a tight shrug. 'The wrong man was put behind bars.'

'Paulo wasn't entirely innocent either.'

'I know that. I don't know what my father's hold over him was but surely he could have said no at some point or just left.' Luka gave a tight shrug, weary from thinking about it. 'He didn't deserve forty-three years, though, and for my father to walk free.'

'You never saw Sophie after she left for Rome?'

'Never,' Luka said. 'It is like she disappeared...'

'I am sure she still visits her father.'

Luka nodded. 'Maybe I *should* go and visit him.'

He was older now—he could face Paulo...

Perhaps he could visit him and ask after his daughter.

Maybe he and Sophie deserved a second chance because, as sure as hell, the years hadn't dimmed the memory. Absence really did make the heart grow fonder because Luka was in the agony of recall again.

And still angry again at her words towards him.

He had never compared her to *her* father.

Paulo was no innocent—he knew full well what two visits from him meant.

Never would he have thrown that at Sophie.

She wasn't like her father, though, Luka thought. She was as volatile and explosive as Rosa.

'I'm going to look her up again,' he said to Angela. 'I will go and see Paulo and make my peace with him.'

'And ask where his daughter is?' Angela smiled.

'I have an earring that needs to be returned!' He smiled; he hadn't expected to smile today but he did. It hurt to be back here but it had cemented some things in his mind.

He and Sophie deserved another chance.

'She might be married,' Angela said. 'She might—'

'Then it's better to know,' he said.

It was the not knowing that killed him.

It hurt too much to be here, Luka thought. He wanted the future, he wanted to explore if there was still a chance for him and Sophie, so he drained his coffee and stood.

'I'm going to head back.'

'Do you want to go through his things first?'

'Just take what you need,' Luka said. 'Get rid of the rest.'

'His jewellery?' Angela said. 'Don't you want that at least?'

'No.' Luka shook his head. He was about to

tell Angela to sell it and keep what she made but then he hesitated—no doubt his father's jewellery hadn't all come by honest means and he did not want Angela in trouble for handling stolen goods.

'I will drop it in to Giovanni on the way to the airport,' Luka said, referring to the local jeweller 'He can melt it down or whatever.'

Angela led him up the stairs and into Malvolio's bedroom.

There was nothing he wanted from here.

He opened up a box and stared at his father's belongings with distaste and then Luka's heart stopped still in his chest and then started beating again, only faster than it had been before.

'Can I have a moment?' he said, and somehow managed a vaguely normal voice. He didn't even see Angela leave but she must have because a moment later he looked up from the jewellery box and she was gone, the door had been closed and he was alone.

Luka watched his hand shake a fraction as it

went into the heavy wooden box and pulled out a simple gold cross and chain.

Yes, he remembered Rosa.

Luka had heard in court how things worked and knew that her necklace must have been taken as a souvenir after her death.

Did Paulo know? Luka wondered.

He looked at the door.

Angela too?

He felt sick as he started counting dates in his head. Yes, he remembered Rosa shouting down the hallway, telling Malvolio that it would be over her dead body before she gave up her home.

The next memory?

Her funeral. Paulo, holding a smiling Sophie, who, at two years old, had had no real idea how sombre the day had been.

He remembered his father delivering the eulogy, telling the packed church how he would support his friend and little Sophie.

Even though he had surely been responsible for Rosa's death?

Was that why Paulo had always said yes to his father? Was that the hold that he'd had over him? Had Paulo done whatever had been asked of him just to keep Sophie safe from the same fate?

Poor man.

Luka had always considered Paulo weak.

Now he glimpsed Paulo's fear. He had done whatever it had taken to protect his child, and Luka knew that he had to help free him.

He would get his lawyers onto it this very day, Luka swore there and then. He would get an apartment in Rome and work for however long it took to secure his release.

There would be no contacting Sophie, though, Luka knew.

There could be no second chance for them now.

He knew Sophie well enough, and she would never forgive him if she knew that it had been his father who had killed her mother.

Never.

The glimmer of hope he had just started to kindle, the fleeting hope for some reconciliation with Sophie, died then as Luka pocketed the necklace.

All he could do for her now was fight to set her father free.

CHAPTER NINE

'I SAW LUKA.'

Sophie had always known that she might hear those words one day but when Bella actually voiced them, for a long moment Sophie did not know how to react.

So much so that she said nothing and just lifted her side of the mattress and carried on making the huge king-size bed.

Sophie had known that Bella wanted to speak with her. As well as sharing a very small flat in Rome, they worked as maids in Hotel Fiscella—a luxurious hotel in the very heart of Rome.

The manager, Marco, had, at first, refused to put them together, knowing that they came from the same Sicilian town. However, when a gap in the roster had given him no choice, Sophie and Bella had set out to prove him wrong. They worked very well together, although they chatted a lot!

Now, though, Sophie was silent.

'I just saw him in the elevator when I went to collect the guest list for our floor.'

'He's not on our list? Sophie checked in horror, but thankfully Bella shook her head.

'Looking at the way he was dressed and held himself, he would be on one of the top floors,' Bella said, and that told Sophie he was doing well.

The hotel was indeed luxurious but the top floors were reserved for the rich and famous.

It had been five years since Sophie had last seen him.

Five years since that walk on the beach.

She knew that Malvolio had died a few months ago. Her father had been diagnosed as terminally ill on the very same day that she had heard the news. After that she had read that Luka had bought an apartment in Rome and now lived between here and London.

Sometimes Sophie was nervous that she might see him in the street, that she would face him in her maid's uniform when she had sworn she could do better without him. That she might face him in the street was bad enough, but knowing that he was at the hotel was far too close for comfort.

'Why would he stay here when he has an apartment?'

'I don't know,' Bella said. 'But it was definitely him.'

When they had read that Luka Cavaliere had purchased a residence Sophie and Bella had even gone to the library to use the computers and had done a virtual tour of the apartment. It had been a foolish thing to do because Sophie found she could picture herself there and all too often did.

'Did he recognise you?' Sophie asked, but Bella just laughed.

'As if he would even glance at a maid! Though I stood behind the bellboy's trolley just in case he looked over.' she admitted. 'But he didn't.'

'I don't want him to see me like this,' Sophie said in sudden panic. 'I don't want him to see that I am still a chambermaid. What if I have to deliver a meal to his room?'

'Don't feel ashamed.'

'I'm not,' Sophie said. 'I just don't want to give him the satisfaction of seeing how little I have moved on.'

'You won't see him. I heard him say he was going back to London this afternoon.'

'Good.'

'What else do you want to know?' Bella asked.

'Nothing.' Sophie shook her head. 'I don't even want to think of that man.'

It was all that she did, though.

Every night when she fell, exhausted, into bed he was there, waiting for her in her dreams. Every morning she awoke cross with her subconscious and how readily it forgave Luka, for her dreams varied from sweet memories of a sun-drenched childhood to a torrid recall of their one passionate afternoon.

They finished making up the bed in silence and Bella went in to do the bathroom while Sophie dusted the flat surfaces of the hotel suite.

Sophie didn't want to ask questions; she wanted to shrug her shoulders and carry on with her day as if a bomb hadn't just dropped in her world, but, of course, that wasn't possible.

She walked into the bathroom and Bella smiled in the mirror that she was polishing when she saw her friend hovering in the doorway.

'Who was he saying it to?' Sophie asked. 'Who was he speaking with?'

'A woman.' Bella's voice was gentle yet the words hurt so much.

'Was she beautiful?' Sophie asked, and Bella screwed up her nose. 'I didn't really notice.'

'I want the truth, Bella,' she said.

Her friend nodded. 'Yes, she was beautiful.'

'Did she have a name?'

'He called her Claudia.'

'And how did he look?' Sophie asked.

'He looked well.'

'Very well?'

'Well, the last time I saw him he was just out of prison so, of course, he looked better than that.'

Sophie knew her friend was trying to down-play things for her.

'His hair is longer now but still very neat. He still has that scar over his eye.'

'Did he look happy?' Tears were in Sophie's eyes as she asked the question, though she never let them fall. It was ridiculous that the man she hated, the man that had caused her family so much pain could still move her so much. That jealousy could rise in her just knowing Luka was carrying on as he always had—dating and living his life—while she Bella worked as maids in a hotel and could barely make ends meet.

'Luka never really looked happy,' Bella said. 'That, at least, is the same.'

Sophie was quiet.

Bella was right—to others he never looked happy. He was sullen and dark but with her he had laughed and smiled.

She had been privy to such a different side of him.

Knowing that Luka had been here in the hotel had Sophie on edge all day, and it was a relief to get away from work.

All she wanted to do was go home and sleep but instead she changed out of her maid's uniform and into a skirt and a T-shirt and then took the bus. She had to stand nearly all the way to the prison infirmary her father had been moved to.

Once there she put on a ring that had belonged to Bella's mother and signed the visitors' book.

Her bag was searched and she was patted down and then she was allowed in.

'Sophie!' Paulo's face lit up when he saw her walk onto the ward. 'You don't have to come and see me every day.'

'I want to.'

Now that he was in the infirmary, visits could be daily, and Sophie knew full well that he had little time left.

'How is Luka?' Paulo asked.

Her father's mental health had deteriorated throughout the trial and by the time he'd got to Rome he'd been a shadow of himself. He had never been a strong man, and was an exhausted man now.

Sophie just wanted him to know a little peace so she had lied to her father over the years and pretended that she was with Luka.

'He's busy with work.' Sophie smiled, grateful that her father was easily confused and very forgetful. 'He says hello and that he will try to come in and visit you soon.'

'Bella?'

'She's still working at the hotel.'

It was the same questions most days and Sophie knew the routine well. She took out some fruit she had bought for him. A lot of her money went on bringing in Paulo treats, even though she couldn't afford to.

'This is too expensive,' her father said, when she gave him a large bowl of raspberries, which had always been his favourite fruit. When she'd been growing up, they had been a very rare treat.

'Luka can afford it,' she said, and the bitter edge to her voice had her father frown, and Sophie did her best to rectify her small outburst. 'He's a good man,' she said.

'If he is such a good man, why hasn't he married you?' Paulo asked.

'I've told you that,' Sophie said. 'He knows how much I want you to walk me down the aisle. We are waiting for that day when you are released…'

It was never going to happen. Paulo did not have long left, maybe a few weeks of life, yet his jail sentence was forty-three years.

'I want to see you married in the same church your mother and I were,' Paulo said.

'I know that you do.' Sophie smiled. 'It will happen one day.'

'Maybe,' he said, and Sophie swallowed back tears at the sudden brightness in his voice. 'The director said this morning that things are looking hopeful.'

'Of course there is hope,' she said, and squeezed his frail hand.

'We will know next Wednesday if I am going to get out.'

Sophie looked up and smiled as a nurse came over.

'The director wants to speak with you, Sophie.'

'Thank you,' Sophie said, and stood. 'I'll be back soon,' she said to Paulo, and walked with the nurse, assuming that she was going to get a health update.

She was led through the prison infirmary and to a corridor of offices and there she met a tired-looking woman, who gave Sophie a warm smile and offered her a seat.

'He's more confused than ever,' Sophie said. 'Now he thinks he is getting out of here on Wednesday.'

'He might be getting released,' the director said, and for a moment Sophie wondered if the chair had been moved for it felt as it the ground had just given way.

'Your father's hearing has been brought forward. We have signed all the forms and have done all we can for him at this end.'

'I don't understand—I didn't even know there was to be a hearing.'

'We are hoping that your father can be released on compassionate grounds. He is no threat to anyone, really he is too weak to go to anywhere other than a hospital or be nursed in your home.' She gave a small shrug. 'Now it is up to the judge to decide but the lawyer who is working on his case is a very good one.'

'I didn't even know there was a lawyer looking out for him.'

'When patients come into the infirmary and their condition is terminal, we try to have their cases reassessed.'

'Why wasn't I told this was happening?'

'It all came about very speedily. When Legal looked at his file they thought there might a possibility for a mistrial but your father does not have time for that. It was thought best to try to get him released on compassionate grounds.' She smiled at Sophie. 'I don't want to get your hopes up but I think in just a few days you might well be able to take your father home.'

Sophie smiled.

It was wonderful news, unexpected and amazing.

And yet it was terrifying too.

She had built a world in her father's mind. One where she lived with Luka in a beautiful flat in Rome, not a scruffy apartment that she and Bella shared.

She had told her father that Matteo and Luka were still friends, which they were, according to the business press, but she hadn't seen him in years.

The only truth she had told was that Bella worked at Hotel Fiscella, only because once Bella had had to visit on her behalf and had worn a coat over her uniform, which her father had seen.

Paulo was confused enough not to question too many things and there was a lot that he didn't remember.

He simply believed that Luka had kept his word and had got engaged to his daughter.

How could she tell her dying father it had all been a lie?

How could she tell him that she had nothing and that, apart from her friend, she had no one?

'I called you in,' the director continued, but it was as if Sophie was hearing from a distance, 'so that you can start to make plans for his release.'

Sophie managed to thank the director and she even went in to kiss her father goodbye. Once outside again, though, she ran from the hospital and took the crowded bus. When she got off, she raced along the cobbled streets and up the small stairwell, where she wrenched open the iron security door and called out to her friend.

'What?' Bella asked, when she saw her stricken face.

'Pa may be being released...'

Bella let out a shocked gasp. 'That's fantastic news.'

'I know that but how can I bring him here when I have told him that I am engaged to Luka, that we live in a beautiful home?'

'You can't tell him the truth,' Bella said. 'Your

father deserves to die knowing that his daughter will be looked after.' Bella's eyes filled with tears. 'My mother didn't know that peace. I think that night Malvolio got released and sent me to work had her go to her grave with a broken heart. It's not going to happen to your father.'

'Oh, so I just produce a luxury apartment? I could just get a photo of Luka, perhaps, and blow it up and sit him in a chair. I know my father is confused but he's not mad...'

'No,' Bella said. 'You are to go and see Luka and tell him that he owes you this much...after the way he shamed you, after all that he said in court, he can damn well go along with things for a while.'

'Do you think I could pull it off?' Sophie said, but then shook her head. 'I can't face him like this.'

'You won't have to,' Bella said. 'I can still sew, I can make you the most sophisticated, elegant woman he has ever seen. You can blow those London women out of the water. He will eat his own words.'

Sophie thought for a moment. 'Luka *could* do it,' Sophie agreed. 'He's a Cavaliere after all. They better than anyone know how to lie under oath.'

CHAPTER TEN

'COULD YOU DIRECT me to Luka Cavaliere's office?'

Sophie stood at a large reception desk and did everything she could to keep the slight tremble from her voice. She was determined to get this right, even if it meant practising her cool façade on the receptionist

'Is he expecting you, Ms...?'

'No, he's not expecting me.' Sophie shook her head. 'If you could just tell me what floor he is on...'

'I'm sorry, but Mr Cavaliere won't see anyone without an appointment.' There was just a slight *something* about the receptionist's voice when she said his name. Her words were tinged with affection and Sophie was quite sure she knew the reason for that.

'For me he would make an exception.' Sophie stared the woman down but it didn't work.

'There *are* no exceptions.' The receptionist smiled her pussycat smile and Sophie glanced at her name badge.

Amber.

'Excuse me,' Amber said as her telephone rang, 'but I need to take this call.'

Sophie stood there as she was summarily dismissed. The beautiful receptionist picked up the phone and started talking but when she had completed the call she blinked, as if surprised to see that Sophie was still there.

'Can I help you?' She frowned.

'You can, Amber,' Sophie responded. 'Please let Mr Cavaliere know that his fiancée is here and that she wishes to see him.'

'His fiancée?'

Sophie watched two spots of colour spread over the woman's cheeks and her cold blue eyes glance down at Sophie's ring finger. 'That's right!' Sophie was the one smiling a pussycat smile now. 'If you could let him know...'

'And your name is…?'

Sophie didn't respond to the question. Luka would know exactly who she was. She pictured his expression when he took the call that would tell him she was back in his life.

A little flustered, the receptionist picked up the phone and relayed the news that Mr Cavaliere's fiancée was there and then gave Sophie a guarded smile. 'I've told his PA and she's going to speak with Mr Cavaliere. If you'd like to take a seat…'

Sophie walked across the elegant foyer to the large leather sofas. She caught sight of herself in the mirror and was relieved for all the effort that she and Bella had made to get to this day.

Bella had, as it turned out, been raiding the bins that they emptied at the hotel for years. Anything that one of the rich guests had thrown out she had squirrelled away.

Beneath Bella's bed were two boxes packed with luxurious clothes.

'This one,' Bella had told her as she held up an ivory silk dress, 'had a little lipstick on the front. She couldn't even be bothered to send it to be dry-cleaned. And these...' She held up some stunning stilettoes. 'They needed to be reheeled, that is all.'

There were coats, jackets, skirts, even night-dresses.

Together they had selected her wardrobe for today and with Bella's skilled hands the rather large ivory dress now clung to Sophie's ripe figure.

The shoes had been reheeled and Sophie's toes had been painted to match her fingernails.

She had flown into London that morning on the red-eye and would be flying back tonight.

The little money they had been saving to fly her father's body, on his death, back to Bordo Del Cielo they had decided to spend on making his last days a dream come true.

Who would guess that Sophie's regular clothes and shoes were in a hired locker at the airport?

Luka must never know.

She had been to a hairdresser's to have her hair put up and then she had changed into the dress

Bella had made for her and gone to the make-up counter at an exclusive department store.

She stood as the receptionist came over. 'Mr Cavaliere says you are to go straight up. I'll walk you to the elevator.'

Sophie wanted to turn and run, to ask for a couple of minutes to check her make-up, or for a glass of water for her very dry mouth, but instead she nodded and crossed the foyer.

His office was on the twenty-third floor and her stomach seemed to have been left on the ground as she sailed closer to him.

The elevator doors opened and Sophie was met by a tearful woman who told her that she was the final straw and then let her know that her fiancé was a cheating bastard...

'You can tell him when you go through that his assistant just resigned!'

Sophie merely smiled.

Ah, Luka, she thought, just a little glad for the chaos she had made for him.

Like a witch, she walked through the corridors of his life, delivering little hexes.

She looked around for a moment, taking his world in. There was a large walnut desk, which presumably had been his assistant's because a computer was on and there was half a cup of coffee by its side, as well as a mirror.

There was the quiet hum of the air-conditioning and fresh floral displays stood on the side tables. The carpet was thick beneath her feet—luxury at every turn.

And there, behind that closed door, Sophie knew, was Luka.

The last time she had knocked on his door he had opened it holding a shirt over his cut and naked from the hips up.

She doubted she'd be so lucky again.

She refused to let him glimpse her nervousness by hesitating and she knocked confidently on the door.

'Come in.'

Confidence faded as, after years of self-imposed abstinence her senses momentarily flared in false hope at the return of his voice.

Still, Sophie barely recognised her hand as

it reached for the handle on the door, the nails glossy and painted, and it wasn't shaking, as she had thought it would be.

She was ready to face him.

For her father she would get through this.

Into his office she stepped and Sophie stood for a brief slice of time, accepting that again they shared the same part of the planet.

It must be difficult for him also, Sophie knew, and that was confirmed when he didn't turn around. She gave them both a moment to acclimatise to the other's presence—the air was a little thicker there and made no room for the rest of the world.

Still he did not turn and so she spoke to his straight back and broad shoulders.

'Your assistant asked me to pass on the message that she's just resigned. Apparently I'm the final straw.'

Don't turn around, she wanted to warn him.

Not just yet.

Don't let my heart see you until it's beating slowly again, but of course it was too late. Slowly he turned and she met navy eyes that, Sophie knew, were better served warm. Today, though, she was grateful they were cold, for it allowed her to maintain a necessary distance when instinct told her to run, though not from him.

It would actually, Sophie thought, be easier to run across the room and hurdle the desk in her tight dress. It would be far more natural to be in his arms than to simply stand in a room apart from him.

He offered her a seat and she took it.

She told him the reason that she was there— that her father might be being released and of the lies she had told about them.

He pushed every button and so, despite her very best efforts to stay cool, within a few moments she was standing, backed against the desk by him and jabbing her fingers in his chest, telling him that he would do whatever it took to make things right for her father. That he would be her fake fiancé, that he owed her that much.'

Surprisingly, he agreed, but then he told her he would *never* marry her. In fact, he spelt it out. 'I will agree to be your fake fiancé but never your fake husband. Know that now, or get the hell out.'

There was a brief stand-off but finally Sophie sat.

'Do you want a drink?' Luka offered, and reached for the phone. 'I can have some lunch sent up...' He frowned in slight annoyance when his call wasn't immediately answered.

'She resigned,' Sophie reminded him as he replaced the receiver.

'So she did.'

'You could perhaps ring down to Amber,' Sophie said. 'I'm sure she'd be only too happy to assist Mr Cavaliere...'

Perhaps because he heard the disdain in her voice Luka gave a soft, mirthless laugh.

'Have you slept with every woman in this building?' Sophie asked.

'All the good-looking ones,' Luka said, and then shrugged. 'I don't have to explain myself to you.' He stood. 'We'll go and get lunch.'

'I don't want to go out for lunch and sit and reminisce. I want to talk...'

'Sophie, I can assure you that I don't want a cosy lunch and a trip down memory lane. I have a meeting at two that I need to be back for and I'd like to have eaten by then.'

They took the elevator down and Sophie smiled a pussycat smile again at Amber as they walked through the foyer.

'You've got a nerve coming here and calling yourself my fiancée,' Luka said. He was furious that she could, within the space of half an hour, completely disrupt his life. Amber was sulking, Tara was gone and now, given he had just agreed to be her fiancé, the next few weeks would be a sexless hell, lying in bed beside her.

'I have nerves of steel,' Sophie said.

Almost.

Until she'd gone to Rome, she had hardly been out of Bordo Del Cielo and now she was in a foreign city with a man who was so familiar he felt encoded. It seemed wrong not to touch, not to hold hands, but instead to walk painfully apart down the busy street.

They entered a restaurant and were led through to the back—clearly he came here often because they greeted him by name. The waft of the aroma of herbs and garlic made her feel a little sick.

There was a flurry of menus but Luka shook his head. 'No wine.'

'Am I business?' Sophie checked, as the wine waiter walked off.

'If you were business,' Luka said, 'there would be the finest red breathing now.'

'If I were pleasure?'

'Champagne in bed,' Luka said. 'Just one glass for me, though. I'd have to get back to work.'

'So too would Amber?' Sophie flashed.

'I always give her the afternoon off afterwards,' Luka retorted. 'I'm nice like that.'

She was angry and more so when she saw that Luka was ordering for her—no doubt he didn't think her capable.

'I can order for myself,' she flared.

'I'm sure you can,' Luka said, 'but I have about thirty-two minutes before I need to get back, I'm hungry, angry and I'm guessing you still eat pasta... This isn't a nice lunch, Sophie, this is sustenance because I didn't have time for breakfast.'

'Why was that?' She couldn't resist raising her eyebrows and then she knew she had gone too far because he leant across the table and put her straight back in her place.

'Don't ask me about these last years Sophie. You could have been in them, you chose not to be.' The waiter came back with two bowls of pasta and Sophie sat bristling as he refilled her water.

She never cried.

Never.

She almost did now, she could feel this sting at the back of her nose. Oh, it wasn't quite bread and water. But almost. She got pasta and thirty-two minutes of his precious time—she got his attention, but the irritated version of it.

How might it have been?

'So you work as an events planner?' Luka checked. 'Full time?'

'No.' Sophie shook her head. 'I mean yes, but

I have cleared my diary, given that he might be getting out of prison...'

'That must have cheered your clients.'

'I handed them over to a friend in the business.'

'Good,' Luka said.

They talked business, or rather they discussed cold facts.

He told her about his Rome apartment and while she was there he called the management and told them his fiancée would be moving in.

'Over the weekend,' Luka said, but as Sophie went to protest he hung up.

'The judgment isn't till Wednesday.'

'You'll need time to get your bearings and move some of your things over. Give your name at Reception and they will give you a key and help with your luggage. I'll be there Tuesday night...'

'Maybe we should wait to see what happens in court.'

'We'll just have dinner, sort out some final details...' Luka glanced at the time. 'I need to get back.'

Sophie went to stand but he gave her a look that had her halt. 'What are you doing?'

'I was going to walk back with you.'

'Why?' Luka asked. 'We have said all that we need to for now. I will see you on Tuesday night. I have a lot to sort out between now and then. Just give me your number in case I need to contact you.'

'I'll contact you.'

'Fine.'

He walked out of the restaurant and Sophie sat there, watching him disappear into the street, and not once did he look back.

'Could I have the bill?' Sophie asked, but the waiter shook his head.

'It's been taken care of'

She looked at the businessmen ordering coffee, at the groups of laughing friends sharing desserts and the loving couples taking their time over a leisurely lunch with wine.

It was a long ride back to Heathrow.

Yet it felt like a very quick flight back to Rome.

She arrived at Fiumicino airport, where Bella was waiting for her.

'*Credeva voi*?' Bella asked.

'Yes, he believed me,' Sophie answered.

Luka believed she was rich.

Luka believed she was successful.

Even at her very best, he still did not want her.

CHAPTER ELEVEN

'THIS COULD HAVE all been yours,' Bella said, as they walked through Luka's apartment in Prati on the eve of judgment day for her father.

They had picked up the keys in Reception and had declined help with her luggage, but as they'd let themselves in both had been blown away.

Yes, they had seen it online, but walking through it was breath-taking. The tall arched windows were beautifully dressed in heavy fabric. The décor was a mixture of antiques yet there was every modern luxury.

'There's an internal elevator,' Bella said. 'Shall we go up to the rooftop?'

Sophie shook her head. 'I'll explore there later.'

It was agony to be here and to know it was his.

Bella had been busy and now in the wardrobe in the main bedroom hung elegant dresses, skirts and jackets and some shoes. Bella had lent Sophie her mother's heavy silver hairbrush and that was in the large bathroom, along with expensive toiletries they had bought. But even with everything they had managed to cobble together over the last few days, even with all their resources pooled and their savings almost spent, it was just a tiny drop in the ocean compared to Luka's obvious wealth.

'Doesn't it make you feel jealous?' Bella pushed.

'I chose not to go to London with him, remember. Anyway, who knows what would have happened if I had gone? We might not have got on,' Sophie pointed out 'One romantic afternoon doesn't mean that we would have lasted a lifetime. And, anyway, I want nothing that has Malvolio's name attached to it.'

'Luka works hard.'

'We work hard,' Sophie said. 'The only difference is we didn't get a step up on the ladder. Our parents didn't give us a share in a hotel to kick our careers off.'

It was easier to resent him, to sound jealous. It was far easier then admitting the truth—that she missed him so much, every single minute of every single day.

And as for the nights...

'What time is he getting here?' Bella asked.

'Any time now,' Sophie said. 'We're going out to dinner to make sure our stories match.'

'Well, just be as expensive as the women where we work. Don't say sorry to staff and don't...' Bella gave her a smile. 'You'll be fine. Oh, I got you a present. Actually, two...'

'Bella!' Sophie scolded when she saw the latest phone. 'We can't afford this.'

'Yes, we can. You can hardly pretend to be an event planner and not even have a phone. When you're done with Luka, I want it if you don't.'

'What's this?' She opened the second present, which was a heavy bottle filled with very expensive perfume. 'Bella...'

'What woman wouldn't have perfume in the bathroom.'

'We didn't have the money for that.'

'Oh, well…'

'You stole this?'

'Yes, I did,' Bella said. 'And I don't feel guilty and I don't feel ashamed. If that's the worst thing I do then I am glad to do it for you.'

Sophie opened the perfume and sprayed it on her wrist and then squirted Bella, who laughed but then it faded.

She had a question of her own.

'Did he say anything about Matteo?'

'Nothing.'

'I thought they were in business together…'

'We really didn't talk that much.'

'I'm scared I'm going to find out that Matteo is married. I know he must think I'm still a whore.'

'Matteo paid for you,' Sophie pointed out.

There was so much shame for them both.

'I still think about him all the time,' Bella admitted. 'Do you think he remembers me?'

'Of course he must,' Sophie said. 'But it was years ago, Bella. If seeing Luka again has taught me anything it is that people move on. Luka is busy with his life, his women. He has long since moved on from those days. So too must we. When all this over, you and I are going to chase our dreams. I don't care what it takes but you are going to go design school and I'm going to have a career.'

'On the ships.'

'Who knows?' Sophie said. 'But I'm not going to spend the rest of my life mourning Luka. I want this over and done with.'

'I'm going to go,' Bella said.

'Thank you.'

Bella forced a smile. 'I want all the details. Imagine you and Luka sharing a bed after all this time...'

Sophie smiled as her friend left but alone she walked nervously around the apartment. The bedroom mocked her, the bed mocked her. It was hard to believe that soon she would be lying in there at night with Luka. That wasn't all that upset her. It wasn't just the thought that he had lain in this bed with others that had bile rising like a volcano.

It was that Luka had had a life, a good one.

But without her.

Alone she walked around and then pulled back the antique gate and stepped into the elevator, it was small but luxurious, and she stepped out to a view that under any other circumstances would have taken her breath away.

Now, again, she was close to tears.

Rome glittered before her, the view better than any from the hotel because you were actually in it. She could hear the noise from the street below and see the Colosseum and the Vatican. The light was fading and soon the streets would pulse with nightlife yet it was not this view she craved.

She had never ached to be back in Bordo Del Cielo till now—there were too many dark memories there. Since seeing Luka, though, she craved to be there. She wanted to get back to her secret cove and to be near water that was so clear and cool that it took the sting out of summer.

Unable to bear it, Sophie headed back down but there was no relief to be had there, for having worked out a room for her father she walked

down the main corridor and peered into the bedroom she would share with Luka.

The room was magnificent, better than the
presidential suite at the hotel where she worked.

The furnishings were heavy and masculine and
it would take more than a silver hairbrush and a
few dresses in the wardrobe to detract from the
male energy that stopped her from going in.

The bed was wide, dressed in muted jewelled
tones, and she could not imagine herself lying
there with him.

Worse, she tormented herself by imagining him
lying there with another woman.

'Sophie?' His deep voice made her jump and
then spin around on her new high heels.

'I didn't hear you come in.'

'Did you expect me to knock?'

'Of course not.' She could hardly bear to meet
his gaze. She had seen him angry, she had seen
him arrogant and aloof, but she had never seen
him like this—there were lines fanning from his
eyes and his mouth was grim, his complexion
tinged grey, and his tension palpable.

He looked as if he was dreading this just as much as she was.

'Where do you want to go for dinner?' he asked.

'We could have something to eat here.'

'I would guess that we'll be eating here rather a lot,' Luka said. 'If your father gets off, I doubt we'll be going out very much.'

'I don't expect you to be here all the time,' Sophie said. 'We can say that you're busy with work.'

'He's dying, Sophie,' Luka said. 'And if I were engaged to you, if I did love you, your father knows that I would do more than put in a few cameo appearances.'

'Of course.'

'I'll give you a tour,' he offered, but Sophie shook her head.

'I already know my way around.'

'Have you organised a nurse for him?'

'I thought it better to wait and see what happens tomorrow,' Sophie said, although the truth was there was no way she could afford a private nurse for her father.

'I'm going to go to court in the morning,' Luka said. 'I'll text you with what's happening.'

'Why would you go to court?'

'To save you from having to go,' Luka said, and with that simple sentence her heart just about folded in on itself because that was the type of man she had lost. This was what being loved by Luka would mean. 'Have you any idea how big it is going to be tomorrow with the press and everything?' he checked.

'I'm starting to,' Sophie said. 'I saw on the news that the press are already camping out by the court.'

'They think he's going to be there when the ruling is made,' Luka said. 'Hopefully he can slip out of the infirmary before the press work it out. Is there anything else that I need to know?'

'I don't think so. We can talk over dinner.'

'I've changed my mind about dinner,' he said.

'Where are you going?' Sophie asked, as he went to walk out.

'What the hell does it have to with you?' he asked.

'If we're supposed to be engaged...'

'The games begin tomorrow, Sophie.' He came right up to her face. 'Tomorrow we lie in that bed, tomorrow we pretend that we care. I've just realised that tonight I don't have to even pretend that I like you, so I won't. I intend to enjoy my last night of freedom before *my* sentence begins.'

He walked off and Sophie knew she should hold her tongue but it had never been her forte. 'Oh, I'm sorry to have thrown such a spanner into your charmed life.'

'Charmed?' Luka turned. 'Tell me, Sophie, what part of my life exactly is charmed? I've worked eighteen-hour days for this. You talk as if it has been handed to me on a plate.'

'The share in a hotel from Daddy was a rather nice start.'

'He had nothing to do with it. I worked for that myself,' Luka said. 'What I didn't say in court was that I knew for years that my father was rotten to the core and that your father was his yesman. So, tell me more about this charmed life, Sophie. When I came back to London I practically had to go on my knees to my partners at the hotel. Six months in prison takes some explaining. Do you really think my colleagues embraced me on my return? Do you not think that I had to prove over and over that I could be trusted?'

She stood with pale lips as he told her how things had been for him.

'Do you not think that when somebody looks me up and finds out that I was in prison, awaiting trial, for six months that it doesn't slur my name? I took nothing from my father. I have done everything I can to make right what he did. I handed back everything that man gave me. The only thing I couldn't return was the education. You can't unlearn things unfortunately but God knows there are things I've tried to forget...'

He was talking about them, Sophie knew it. He was back in his bed and taking her for the first time with his eyes. 'I washed my hands of Bordo Del Cielo. I only came back that time to rid myself of you once and for all. I should never have opened that door to you!' Even before she could move he grabbed her wrist. 'Slap me again...' Luka warned.

'And you'll slap me back?' Sophie challenged, and she didn't understand because he almost smiled.

Yes, he almost smiled because on so many levels she matched him and in so many ways he adored her. How he would love to end this row in a different way, to kiss her right now into submission, yet he refused that pleasure for himself.

'Slap me again,' he amended, 'and before the fingermarks have faded the engagement will be off and you can tell your father why if you must. I mean it, Sophie, and you should know that I don't give second warnings.'

She stood there and he had won but even as he passed the finish line he kept on sprinting.

'I'm going out now and I'm going to be with a woman who does not question, a woman who is sweet and warm...'

'Give Claudia my love,' Sophie spat, and hoped that the fact she knew his lover's name meant that she sailed past him on shock value alone, but Luka just grinned at the jealous snarl to her voice.

'Claudia?' Luka checked.

'You were with her at Hotel Fiscella.'

'Because Matteo and I are thinking of buying it,' Luka said, and Sophie was grateful that she had handed in her notice as she realised how close she had come to having Luka as her boss. 'Claudia is one of my lawyers.'

'She was there for the purchase of the hotel?'

'No,' Luka said. 'I hired her to get your father released.'

She stood there frozen to the spot, hating how he was always one step ahead, how this man continued to sideswipe her.

'Why?' Sophie asked. 'Why would you hire a lawyer to get my father out?'

No, he didn't tell her about the necklace burning a hole in his pocket and the hellish guilt that had made it his mission to see Paulo freed.

'For this moment, Sophie.' Luka lied. 'So that you would come to my office and ask me to be with you. For the pleasure of lying in bed with you and doing *nothing...*' Black was his smile.

'Why do you hate me so much?'

'You'll work it out,' Luka said. 'I'm going out now. I'll see you tomorrow when the real games begin.'

CHAPTER TWELVE

SHE DIDN'T WANT her father to be released.

Sophie decided she must surely be the most terrible daughter in history because at midday, when still nothing had been said on the news, when still the judge had not ruled, she had this brief fantasy that his application would be denied and she could walk out of the apartment and away from Luka without a single word.

Instead, late in the afternoon, she got a text.

Your father has left the infirmary and will be with you shortly. The judge made his ruling in private for security reasons. It will shortly be announced.

Aside from the hell of what lay ahead, Sophie still wondered what sort of a nightmare her father's release might have been without the well-oiled machine of Luka's life swinging into action.

She saw on the news the crush of reporters both at the court and another group that was now outside the prison infirmary and she shuddered at the thought of her and Bella dealing with this.

Even as the journalists jockeyed for position at the prison gates Paulo was sitting in Luka's home.

'I thought Luka would be here,' Paulo said.

'He was at court,' Sophie said. 'He has been keeping me up to date with all that is going on.'

'It is a beautiful home,' her father said, and then he looked at the view from a huge leather chair. 'Is there a balcony? I would like to breathe fresh air...'

'There's a balcony in your room and there is also a rooftop garden,' Sophie said.

'I would never make the stairs.'

'There's an elevator.' Luka deep voice caught her unawares and again, to the sound of him, she jumped, not that her father noticed.

'Luka!' She heard the sheer joy in her father's voice as he pushed himself to stand and then she watched Luka's eyes briefly shutter as he embraced the old man.

'Thank you,' Paulo said in a heartfelt voice as he took Luka into his arms. 'Thank you for all you did. I know it was you who got me out...'

'Nonsense.' Luka's voice was gruff. 'The judge was right, there were many mistakes made at the trial. You deserve to have your freedom.'

'You knew it was Luka who was behind this?' Sophie checked.

'Of course,' Paulo said. 'There are not many files that just happen to be picked up. I knew that it had to be you.'

'Father?' Sophie frowned because her father sounded far more together than he had in recent weeks. 'Were you pretending to be confused?'

'Sometimes.' He smiled.

'He's not really sick,' Luka said, and then he saw Sophie's horrified expression at the thought that they might be stuck in this lie for ever so he relented. 'That was a joke.'

'Ha-ha,' Sophie said, and then she looked at her father and she knew in her heart that he didn't have long and yet somehow he was here and they were together.

It was agony.

For Paulo the best wine sat breathing up on the rooftop. Sophie had spent the long day waiting for news, cooking her father's favourite pasta sauce, which he ate with relish.

'It tastes of home,' Paulo said. 'Almost.'

She glanced at Luka's plate.

It was untouched.

She watched as Luka poured three glasses and her father reached for his.

'Should you be drinking?' Sophie checked. 'You are on a lot of medication.'

'You are your mother's daughter.' Paulo laughed. 'I just got out of prison.'

'Even so...'

'You worry too much,' Paulo chided.

'Someone has to.'

Luka glanced over at Sophie's slightly bitter retort. She had dealt with so much, that Luka knew—moving so that she could be close to her father, giving up her dreams of working on the cruise liners.

Letting go of them?

Had that been what she had been doing on the beach that night? Luka briefly pondered.

What did it matter now?

The past was closed.

They just had the present to get through and despite Paulo's slight second wind from his release, Luka knew the charade would not play out for long.

'So.' Paulo looked over at Luka. 'What are your plans for my daughter?'

'I learnt a long time ago that it is foolish to make plans on Sophie's behalf,' Luka responded. 'She is her own person.'

He looked at Sophie's tense expression. There was a curl of thought forming but he soon lost that thread because Paulo was making grand plans.

'I'd like to have a party,' Paulo said. 'We never toasted your engagement.'

'There's no need for a party,' Sophie said. 'We don't need a fuss to be made.'

'I would like to celebrate.' Paulo was insistent. 'Just a small gathering.'

He started to cough and Sophie took him inside, leaving Luka sitting out there.

'Please, Sophie,' her father said as she helped him to bed. 'I want some photos for you to keep. I want a night we can all remember...'

She didn't need photos to remember this, Sophie thought as she came out of her father's bedroom.

'He's asleep,' she said.

'Lucky him.' Luka's response was curt. 'I might take one of the spare rooms—' Luka started, but any hope of pulling that particular piece of wool over Paulo's eyes faded as his bedroom door opened.

'Could you bring me my wine from the table?'

'Father!'

'Stop fussing,' Paulo said. 'And can you show me how the radio works? I would like to fall to sleep to music.'

As Sophie headed up to the rooftop garden he smiled at Luka. 'Where do you two sleep?' Paulo checked. 'Just in case I need Sophie in the night. I won't come in, of course. I'll just knock.'

'Sophie sleeps in that room,' Luka attempted. 'I have the main one.'

'Please!' Paulo was laughing as Sophie reappeared with his wine. 'Your fiancé is trying to tell me you have separate rooms! I am not that old-fashioned that you have to pretend.'

'Great!' Luka hissed, as they finally closed the door to his room.

'I told you that he'd never buy us sleeping apart.'

'I just never envisaged the hell it would be.'

Sophie went into the bathroom and undressed. She put on a small nightdress and took a few calming breaths before heading out.

Luka wasn't about to scuttle off to the bathroom to change and was still stripping off as she slipped into bed.

'He wants this party.'

'Then he can have one. I will call Matteo,' Luka said. 'I'll ask him to fly in.'

'He might let it slip that we haven't been together very long.'

'Why would he let it slip?' Luka frowned. 'Matteo knows what is going on, he's a good friend. He knows that this is all just a ruse.'

'You've told him?'

'Why wouldn't I tell him, Sophie? We work together, we are in business together, we grew up together. I don't keep secrets from people who matter to me any more.'

'I could ask Bella.'

'Whatever you want. I'll ring him now.'

'But it's nearly midnight.'

'Yes,' Luka snapped. 'I'm early to bed tonight.'

'Can you go one hour without reminding me about your active sex life?'

'Why does it bother you so much, Sophie?'

She didn't answer.

Luka laughed at her non-reaction and got into bed. He called Matteo and lay chatting to his friend. Yes, it was hell being engaged, he told him, and then he was serious.

'We're going to have a small party for Paulo,' Luka said. 'Will you be able to fly in? Sophie might ask Bella...' There was a pause before Luka spoke again. 'Of course it's not a problem. Bring anyone you choose.'

He hung up.

'He can only make it tomorrow,' Luka said.

'Tomorrow?'

'He has an important meeting to prepare for in Dubai. Is tomorrow a problem?'

'Of course not.'

'Oh, and he's bringing his girlfriend.'

Sophie decided against asking Bella. She knew how crushed she be to see Matteo with another woman.

'I'll keep it simple,' Sophie said, thinking, as she always had to, about money. 'I might just make his favourite meals...'

'Get it catered,' Luka said. 'Today was an exception. I understand you wanted to give him a taste of home tonight but I'm telling you this much—if you were my fiancée you wouldn't have spent the day slaving and making sauce when there are the best restaurants across the street. Get someone to come and dress the garden and organise the music...' He stopped then. 'Sorry, I forget that you're an events organiser.'

Sophie was sure he knew she'd been lying.

'Is he driving you mad yet?' Luka asked, and Sophie gave a reluctant smile, because her father was driving her a little crazy. 'Are you starting to remember why you were only too willing to leave?'

'A bit,' Sophie admitted. 'I am sick of him saying I am just like my mother.'

'She had him under her thumb,' Luka said.

They lay in bed and it felt impossibly awkward, or at least it did for Sophie. Luka seemed completely fine with it. His hand was beneath the sheet and she blinked when she realised he was arranging himself in his underwear, then he saw her shocked look but merely shrugged.

'I've got an erection. I'm just moving it.' He

grinned at her shocked expression. 'Don't worry, I'm not going to come near you.'

'You're in a very good mood.'

'I know,' Luka said. 'I thought it would be hell but I'm really enjoying myself. I like seeing your father free and I love watching you edgy and able to do nothing about it.'

Then he did the cruellest thing.

He kissed her on the tip of her nose and two minutes later he was asleep.

CHAPTER THIRTEEN

LUKA WOKE UP AND for the first morning in his life it was the right face on the pillow next to him.

He examined her beautiful face and he looked at where one breast had fallen out of her nightdress. Their legs were loosely entwined, hers over one of his and beneath the other.

She was loyal, she was fierce and she matched him.

He knew their dance, even if it had only been a short one.

He knew the steps, for their souls were familiar.

And she would never forgive him for what his father had done.

If she did, it wouldn't be for long. In the heat of the moment his father's sins would be raised and then hurled at him in her, oh, so Sicilian way.

And he would not live like that.

He wished it were different.

If he could change one thing about her, would he, though?

It would be like trimming the corner off a work of art, or like removing one letter from the alphabet and watching one's words fall apart.

'Why are you staring at me?' Sophie asked as her brown eyes opened to his.

'Because you're in my bed and there is not much else to look at.' Then his eyes drifted down to her exposed breast and he gave a lazy smile as she tucked herself in.

'See,' Luka said, 'it's rude when I rearrange myself, but not when you do.'

'Hard again, Luka?' Sophie smiled.

'That's for me to know,' Luka answered, and didn't even roll over as she climbed out of bed and went to her wardrobe.

She had no idea what to wear. Bella had made her plenty of stunning clothes but none were very practical for making coffee so instead she took out one of his shirts.

'How's the phobia?' Luka asked. 'Last time

you put on one of my shirts there were ten po-
licemen in the bedroom. You seem remarkably
calm—no flashbacks?'

She didn't bother answering him. Instead, she
went to make coffee and didn't look up when
Luka came through. He was wearing a suit and
looked ready for the office.

'I thought you'd take today off.'

'No.'

'I thought—'

'I have an office here in Rome and I have a lot
of work that needs to be done. Anyway, I thought
it might be nice for you to have a day with your
father, without being on edge with me here.'

'I'm going to take him in some breakfast,' Sophie said.

'The doctor is coming at nine to check up on
him,' Luka said, and he put a credit card on the
bench.

'What's this for?'

'The caterers and things.'

'I can cover that,' Sophie lied. She really had

been intending to spend the day cooking and doing what she could to prepare for tonight.

'Please, don't say you will get this. You asked me to go along with things as if we were together. Well, that is how it would be. Book the caterers, get the garden looking beautiful. I have never heard of your business so I don't know how easy it will be for you to arrange things with no notice. Use my name, you won't have a problem'

She didn't have a single one.

It was strange to have the world at your fingers, courtesy of the Cavaliere name.

Except people didn't jump in fear when she rang and said that she was organising a last-minute gathering; instead, they seemed genuinely happy to help.

And so she enjoyed herself amidst the saddest of times.

The columns of foliage and scented trees were decorated with tiny lights that would come on at sunset. A string quartet had been arranged and the food had Sophie's mouth watering even as she made her selections.

Hearing her father cough and struggle to catch his breath, Sophie knew this would all be over, long before the credit-card bills came in.

'What's this?' Paulo asked.

'A new shirt and suit.' Sophie smiled. 'They just need you to try it on so they can take it in.'

Yes, to Sophie, Luka's life *was* charmed.

And so she had a beautician come to Luka's home and sat on a velvet chair in the bedroom as her thick black hair was spun into heavy ringlets and her eyelids were painted a smoky grey.

'Red lips...' the beautician said, but Sophie shook her head.

In her bag, still there, was her once-used lip glaze.

She wondered if it would all have dried up but, no, it went on easily.

'Just touch it up through the evening,' the beautician said. 'And try not to play with your hair or the curls will drop.'

Sophie chose her dress from the selection Bella had made. A simple black dress that went with the shoes she had worn on the day she had walked into his office was her choice. She tried it on and let out a small hiss of frustration. The front was far too low and as for the back there wasn't one.

Luka walked in as Sophie stood staring in the mirror, trying to fathom if she'd be safe without a bra.

He saw first her back, glossy and brown, with black ringlets snaking down it. He looked down and saw the muscles of her calves drawn lean in high heels and he walked over, anticipating her slight jump as he came into view in the mirror.

'I'm sorry about all this,' Sophie said.

'Don't be sorry.' Luka shrugged. 'I agreed to go along with this. Of course your father would want a special night.'

'Thank you.'

He looked at her lips and told himself he was imagining things because they were the very lips he had kissed that long-ago day. He looked down at the gape of unrestrained cleavage and thick nipples that jutted from the fabric.

'I forgot to pack my backless bra...'

'Those bras are the ugliest things I've ever seen.'

She could feel a shiver on her back, so light she thought it might be his finger, but she realised he was holding a drink with one hand and removing his tie with the other.

It was the nerves on her spine that were leaping in hope.

'I'll change,' Sophie said, turning to go to the wardrobe, except Luka didn't step aside and she walked slap bang into him.

His drink he held steady.

It was her heart that seemed to spill on the floor.

'You'll wear that,' Luka said. 'You'll wear what turns me on.'

'Why?' Sophie demanded. Why the hell would he do this to them?

'Mortification of the flesh,' Luka answered. 'It's my new game.'

He undid his shirt and she could feel the tense pinch of her nostrils as he took it off and she would hold her breath till he headed for the shower.

He didn't, though.

Instead, he went to the wardrobe and took out a clean shirt.

'Aren't you going to shower?'

'There's no time for that.'

'Luka, please...'

'Do I smell?' He came over and lifted his arm and she simply refused to breathe him in. 'No, I showered this morning. You get me in the raw...'

She wanted him clean and sterile—she didn't want his heady scent.

'See?' Luka smiled at her pale face. 'It's a good game. Well, it is for me. I keep forgetting you don't like all that business...' He did up his shirt and Sophie chose to get out.

'I'm going to help my father get ready.'

'No need.' His eyes did not leave her alone for a minute. 'I brought a nurse back with me. Another one will take her place at midnight. They come with the best references and I have done the necessary checks.'

'I take care of my father.'

'Of course you do,' Luka said. 'But as a daughter, not a nurse. I was thinking today that if I had a child, not that I ever will, but if I did I would not want them looking after me in that way. Enjoy him as your father now.'

'I can't afford a nurse.' Her words were shrill, her admission reluctantly dragged through strained lips, but Luka didn't even blink.

'You know,' he drawled, 'they're the first honest words to come out of your mouth. We need to head out there. Matteo and Shandy will be here soon, I believe they're getting engaged in a few weeks...'

'Shandy?' Sophie said, resentment prickling for Bella, for her heart would break when she found out that Matteo was about to get engaged. 'What sort of a name is that? Is he bringing a horse?'

'Oh...' Luka gave a low laugh. 'She's back.'

'Who?'

'The *real* Sophie,' Luka answered. 'I keep glimpsing her but then you tuck her away. Bring her out, Sophie. Don't worry, I can handle her.'

The *real* Sophie took the elevator with him up to the rooftop garden.

Her father was there, thanks to the nurse.

And so too were Matteo and Shandy.

'You've done well,' Luka said.

Sophie had. The garden twinkled with lights, the string quartet was softly playing and the waiters were waiting to pounce.

'It's been so long,' Sophie said, and kissed Matteo's cheek.

'Just not quite long enough,' Matteo said, and Sophie jerked her head back.

He hated her too, only she didn't understand why.

'This is Shandy.' Matteo introduced the glossy blonde and Sophie looked at her. With her long legs and slightly protruding teeth, she actually did slightly resemble a horse.

'Shandy.' Sophie kissed her on both cheeks too and met Luka's eyes.

She would behave, Sophie swore.

The food was delicious.

Porcini mushrooms with black truffle pappardelle, the sauce thick and creamy and mopped up with bread rich with herbs and olives, but, Paulo mused, 'It cannot beat Sicilian *panne*...'

'Nothing beats Sicilian,' Sophie said.

She meant it for Bella, for her friend, she meant it to remind Matteo of the woman who was not here tonight, yet it was Luka's eyes she met as she said it.

'No.' She put her hand over the wine glass as the waiter went to pour.

'Enjoy yourself.' Luka smiled. 'I am.'

He liked the real Sophie; he liked watching her attempt to rein herself in as he invited her to come out.

Both were, both knew, playing the most dangerous of games.

Dessert was pure heaven—thick cassata that was as rich and as liqueur-laced as it had been more than a decade ago when he had denied her that kiss.

And then tiny *cannellonis*, the ricotta tart with lemon, refreshing to the tongue.

'Limoncello.' Paulo smiled as he sipped the

drink of home, and then he stood on frail legs as Sophie sat.

'Tonight makes up for many things,' Paulo said. 'Tonight I sit with old friends and new...' He raised a glass to Shandy, and Luka and Matteo did the same.

The glass felt like lead to Sophie but she raised hers too.

Then she had to listen to her father say how right she and Luka were. That they were simply meant for each other.

'Luka was twelve when his mother died. I remember Sophie crying that night for his pain.' She had forgotten that. Deliberately. To escape the pain, she had avoided their past and now her father walked them both through it.

For appearances' sake Luka's hand was over hers but it was hot and dry and there was no caress from him as her father exposed the love that was lost.

'When we had a party for Luka moving to London, I remember Sophie coming down the stairs.

She had put tissues in her bra. She wanted Luka to notice her...

"'In time,' I told her. But she was fourteen and impatient and did not want to listen to me,' He looked at Sophie. 'Listen to me now. You and Luka's time is now. Don't ever waste it.'

Then it was Luka's turn to speak.

He cleared his throat and thanked their few guests. Out of the corner of her eye Sophie could see that her father was fading. Smiling but fading, and she was so grateful to Luka to have given him this night.

'Paulo, we are so happy to celebrate this night with you. I am very blessed. Some might say that I have a *charmed* life...' He looked at Sophie and with a smile that did not reach his eyes he painted her heart black. 'That is because of you, Sophie...' He offered her his hand and Sophie stood. 'I know you have your ring, but I wanted something to mark this night.'

She opened a box and there was a fine bracelet and she read the inscription:

'*Per sempre insieme.*'

Together for ever.

She wanted to hurl it over the balcony and to the street or throw it across the floor, but instead she handed it to her father, who was putting on his glasses to read what had been written.

'We should go soon,' Matteo said to Shandy.

'Why?' Sophie challenged. 'When we're having so much fun?'

'You could stay here,' Luka offered, but Matteo shook his head. 'It is good to check the hotel out...'

'Where are you staying?' Paulo asked.

'Fiscella,' Matteo answered, and Sophie shivered and hoped that Bella wasn't working there tomorrow. 'Luka and I are thinking of buying it,' he explained to Paulo. 'It is a nice old hotel but it needs a lot of refurbishment. I want to see for myself a few things.'

'Doesn't Bella work there?' Paulo asked, and Sophie tensed, especially when she felt the scrutiny of Luka's gaze.

'She does.'

'Doing what?' Matteo asked.

'She's a chambermaid,' Paulo answered. 'Isn't she, Sophie?'

'Well, I guess it gives her access to a richer clientele.' Matteo's response was surly and, taking Shandy by the hand, he led her to the floor to dance.

'I thought you would wear your mother's earrings tonight,' Paulo said. 'You wanted them for your engagement.'

'They didn't go with the dress.' Sophie's answer was brittle and Luka noted it.

'Come on,' Luka said. 'Dance.'

I don't want to dance with you, she wanted to say. *I don't want to be in your arms because there I might convince myself that this is real.*

He held her at her waist and she could feel his cheek by hers and it was their first dance and had to be their last because it nearly killed her to be back in his arms.

Yet she didn't want their one dance to end—ever.

'Why did you get me that bracelet? Why would you have engraved "Together for Ever"?'

'What did you want me to have inscribed? *"Né tu letu né iu cunsulatu"*?'

She looked right at him with narrowed eyes as he delivered a very apt Sicilian saying—'Neither you happy nor I consoled.'

'Do you need consoling, Luka?' Her smile was mean with seduction.

'Are you happy?' Luka asked, and saw that her smile struggled to stay on. 'Do you miss it?'

'Miss what?' Sophie hissed, yet she knew what was coming and she was right, for he practically echoed Bella's words.

'Everything we could have had.'

'You ended things with me,' Sophie said. 'You came back to Bordo Del Cielo just to say you didn't want to marry me.'

'Oh, you are so good at rewriting history, Sophie,' Luka refuted. 'I ended the old us, we were just starting anew. It was you that ultimately broke things off. You who refused to come to London with me. So,' he asked, 'do you regret it?'

If she said that she did, then she admitted her love. And if she admitted her love, then it made the last years wasted, and that shamed her more than being led to a police car dressed in his shirt.

Instead, she clung to her pride as she fought not to rest her head on his shoulder. 'No.'

'Then you're more of a fool than I thought.'

'Oh, I'm a fool now, am I?' Sophie retorted. 'A peasant and a fool.'

'You'll never let it go, will you? Always you let your temper get the better of you,' Luka said into her ear, and she fumed silently in his arms as one by one he took out her faults and examined them as their bodies swayed to the music and turned the other on. 'Your quick tongue...'

'My slow tongue...' Sophie said, and he laughed a dark laugh at her attempt to change the subject.

Yes, the old Sophie was back.

'It won't work, Sophie.'

'Ah, but it already has,' she said, because she could feel him hard against her and certainly, for Luka's sake, one dance must now become two.

'You should be careful who you tease,' he said into her ear. 'I have no problem sleeping with you and then walking away.'

'You would do that, wouldn't you?'

'Oh, yes,' Luka said. 'So don't play with fire.'

It felt strange to be both angry and turned on, to want and to resist.

'Why do you loathe me?' Sophie asked. 'You have a wonderful life. And why does Matteo hate me?'

'Because I'm boring when I'm drunk,' Luka said. 'I guess I tend to complain about you.'

'And why do you hate me so?'

'Many reasons.'

'Such as?'

'You held what my father did against me. You compare me to him when I never did that to you.'

'My father is a good man.'

'Perhaps, but he is not completely innocent.' He dropped a kiss on her burning shoulder and there was nowhere to hide, no row that could be had in the public arena she had made for them, and resistance was agony.

'Don't make him out a saint,' Luka said.

'I don't.' Sophie closed her eyes as his face came back to her cheek.

'What else?' she asked.

'Your inability to back down, to admit you were wrong,' Luka said, and then he warned her what he was about to do. 'I'm going to kiss you now. I'm going to kiss you and there is nowhere you can go and nowhere you can hide, and I am going to remind you what you let go. You are going to taste what you must now miss every day.'

'A small kiss is hardly going to have me on my knees.'

'Who said small?'

'There are people present. My father...'

'Would he not expect us to kiss at our engagement party? Just pull away when it gets too much...'

'Luka, you seem to think I still want you. I told you, I don't want anyone.'

'Oh, that's right—your phobia...'

He pulled his head back so she could see his black smile.

'When you need me to stop, I shall.'

Sophie blinked. She already needed him to stop and he had barely started, but just the graze of his lips was too much, just the press of his mouth was too dangerous.

He was necessarily cruel.

Necessarily because their mouths needed each other, and it was a relief just to give in to mutual want.

The shiver along her spine this time came from his fingers, and it was Sophie's tongue that caressed his.

Just the tip.

That cool, muscular tip that stroked hers enough to remind their scalding bodies of the fire they'd once made.

'Enough for show,' Sophie said, and pulled back.

Just not enough for them.

'I'm going to see Matteo off.' Luka ran a slow tongue over his lips and tasted her again. 'Your father looks as if he needs to go to bed.'

He left her burning.

As Luka saw their guests off, Sophie took the elevator with her father and the nurse.

'It is good to see you so happy.'

'We are happy, Dad,' Sophie told him, as she saw him to his room. 'You can see how Luka takes care of me. You don't have to worry any more.'

'But I do,' Paulo said, then turned to the nurse. 'Can you excuse us, please?'

The nurse nodded and they walked into his room. 'You have no idea how good that feels,' Paulo said.

'What?'

'To ask for privacy and to be given it. You have made my final days happy, Sophie, but there is more that I want. I need to walk you down the aisle. I want to return to Bordo Del Cielo...'

'The journey will be too much for you.'

'Then I will die returning home to my Rosa.'

'Father...'

'Sophie, don't say no to me. Let me see you and Luka marry in the same church that your mother and I did, now, this weekend. I won't see another one, this much I know...'

How could she say no to him?

'I'll speak to Luka.'

CHAPTER FOURTEEN

SHE WALKED INTO the bedroom. Luka was lying on his side, his back to her and the sheet low on his hips.

She didn't know if he was awake or asleep but she knew that she had to tell him between now and the morning that she had told her father they would marry. She headed into the en suite and started to undress then realised she had left her nightdress in the bedroom. Rather than going back in there, she undressed and wrapped herself in a towel then took off her make-up and brushed her teeth.

Luka was going to be furious, Sophie knew.

But, hell, he must surely understand the impossible situation her father had put her in. He was days away from dying—of course he wanted to go home one last time, of course he would want to see his daughter married to the man she supposedly loved.

Loved?

She didn't love Luka, she abhorred him, Sophie told herself, but then she caught sight of her lying eyes in the mirror as she rinsed her mouth.

Her body loved him, she knew, because it hadn't just been hard work and few hours to spare that had kept her from other men, it had been the utter lack of wanting them when she looked at them. She'd had a few kisses that had tasted of plastic compared to being devoured by the man on the other side of the bathroom door.

She stepped into the bedroom.

'Luka…' Her voice was perhaps a little too quiet for someone who was truly trying to wake another, but when he didn't respond Sophie decided that she'd tell him in the morning, and she slipped out of her dress and panties.

'What?'

He didn't turn and Sophie reached for her nightdress as she spoke. 'It will keep till morning.'

'Tell me now.' He turned then and he wished

he hadn't for despite the darkness he could see her naked body with arms raised as she pulled on her nightdress.

He should turn away quickly, yet he didn't. Instead, in that brief moment everything he'd imagined was verified. He had been trying to ignore her, willing sleep to come before she slipped into bed beside him and now he had to endure another night fighting instinct.

Sophie met his eyes and denied the sexual tension between them. 'My father...' She kept her voice calm. 'I couldn't get out of it.'

'Get out of what?'

'He wants to go back to Bordo Del Cielo as soon as possible. He wants to visit my mother's grave.'

'I'll arrange the flight, you can go with him. I'll make up some excuse about work as the reason I cannot be there. I never want to go back.'

'He wants us both to go with him, though,' Sophie said. His eyes were fixed on hers and her skin prickled with heat as she continued. 'I've said that we will marry this Sunday.'

He said nothing and she stood there awaiting his response.

'Luka?'

'Are you going to stand there all night or get into bed?'

Sophie took a tentative step forward, pulled back the sheet and slipped in.

Her heart was thumping. The tension in the room was almost unbearable—a mixture of fear at his response and a deep, thick arousal. She knew he was turned on, and so too was she; she could not catch her breath, though she tried to keep it even.

'Did you hear what I said about us?'

'I heard.'

'You didn't respond.'

'I have already told you where I stand on that—I will never marry you.'

'But I've told him that we shall.'

'Then you'd better hope that he dies before the service is due to commence.'

'Luka...' Fury bolted her upright but he pulled her down and pinned her.

'What?' he demanded. 'Say what you were going to.'

'You can't mean that.'

'Oh, I mean it,' he said. 'I'll go along with it, I'll go back home with you and get involved with the preparations. I'll say and do all the right things right up until the church but know this—I won't be standing at the altar when you get there, Sophie. You'll be jilted in front of the town.'

'You hate me so much that you'd do that to me.'

'I hate you as much as I want you.'

'That doesn't make sense,' Sophie said, yet even as the words left her lips she had worked out what he meant. He hated her fiercely, judging by the erection now pressing into her thigh.

'I'll make it clearer, then,' Luka said. 'I hate you as much as you want me.'

'But I don't want you. I don't want anyone,' Sophie said. With every cell in her body she lied and she knew he knew it. 'Will you marry me, Luka? I'm not asking for forever...'

'You miss the very point.'

'Luka, can we start again?' Sophie drew in a

breath. 'Can we put the past behind us and start anew?'

'Without examining it?' Luka checked. 'Without accusing?'

'Yes.'

'How very convenient, Sophie, because then you don't have admit you were wrong. You get to wipe the slate clean for as long as it suits you.'

'What does that mean?'

He got up and headed to the safe where her mother's necklace was kept and opened it.

Just hand it to her, he told himself.

Simply give her the benefit of the doubt.

Hand it over to her and see what she says.

'You want a clean slate?' Luka checked.

'Yes,' Sophie said. 'I won't raise what was said in court.'

He stared at the cross and chain; he almost believed she could do it until Sophie spoke on.

'I won't bring up the other women.'

'But. You. Just. Did!' Luka shouted in exasperation, and took out the earring instead of the cross. She was nowhere ready for the truth.

'You're still the fourteen-year-old kid padding her bra.'

'Meaning?'

'You haven't grown up, or rather you haven't moved on.'

'Still the peasant.'

'One row,' Luka shouted, 'one cross word and you hurl the past back at me. So where's the clean slate, Sophie?'

'Keep it down,' she said. 'I don't want my father to hear us row.'

'He can't,' Luka said. 'These walls are soundproof So row away, Sophie, say what you have to. Here...' He tossed her a piece of gold.

Just not the right one.

'My mother's earring.'

'I found it in my bedroom,' Luka said. 'Come on, Sophie, say what you have to.'

'I don't want to row.'

'You want to make love?' Luka checked.

She ran an eye over his naked body and when most might avert their eyes from an angry erection, Sophie frowned.

'I don't think it has love on its mind.'

Uh-oh!

Luka walked over and she refused to flinch as he shredded her flimsy nightdress.

'You'll have sex with me yet you won't go through with the marriage?' Sophie checked.

'Yes,' Luka said. 'And if you knew my reputation you would know many of my girlfriends have complained about the same thing.'

'Ah, but you don't make love to them the way you do with me.'

'You don't know that.'

'I do know that,' Sophie said, and looked right into his eyes. 'Absolutely I do.'

'That's a very confident assumption for someone who's only had sex twice.'

'Once,' Sophie corrected. 'We only did it—'

She never got to finish. His mouth was hard on her hers and he kissed her then as he had wanted to on the dance floor.

He kissed her hard until she was kissing him back, her fingers knotting in his hair.

'Remember, I don't want charity,' Luka said, as his thighs parted her legs.

He made her back down.

With his refusal to go further, he tested their patience to the edge.

'It isn't charity,' Sophie said, as she guided him to her heat.

'Some phobia.'

He exposed her lie and she didn't care, as long as he took her now.

Yet he didn't.

And neither did he leave her hanging on; instead, he knelt up.

'What are you doing?'

'Picking up where we left off.'

He lowered his face to her and confirmed her desire for she was wet and swollen and a moment away from coming to him.

She tried to scramble away from him, but he held her hips down; she wanted them face to face, not this intimate, raw exploration where there was no place to lie.

And, Sophie thought as he pressed his long

tongue in over and over again, she was wrong to berate him for past lovers.

She should handwrite them all thank-you notes because his mouth was sucking on her clitoris now and his fingers were probing her along with his tongue, and she was sobbing as she came to him.

'Luka…'

He was kneeling between her parted legs, pulling them apart when they ached to close in on the orgasm he had just delivered her.

'What?' Luka checked, as he nudged a little way in. 'Do you want to me stop?'

He would.

The bastard would.

'Or,' Luka said, 'I go deeper.'

She could hear the sound of them, feel the tease of him that had her beating below again.

'Just come,' Sophie said.

'I told you, I loathe martyrs.'

He rested on his heels and pulled her hips down and carried on his cruel tease, there but not, in but not enough.

'Or,' Luka offered, 'we could try something different...'

'Like?' Sophie asked, and he suppressed a smile.

He could feel her mounting tension, he was holding down her hips as they rose in his hands.

'Something dangerous,' Luka said, and she nodded her head, set now on a rigid neck.

And so he kissed her like the first time.

When they'd tasted sweet and new.

He toppled onto her as he fully entered her again, and he brushed her wet lips with his as she clawed at his back and then gave in.

They made love.

They might well regret it tomorrow, but that was for then.

Now he kissed her like he only ever would kiss her, and Sophie just drank it in.

She smiled and she pushed back his damp hair just to see him, just to feel it. She stopped fighting and started caressing and they rolled, made love to each other, nipped, sucked and tasted, and came.

And came again.

Guns were down.

Walls were gone.

She accepted his temporary truce as they made up for lost time.

CHAPTER FIFTEEN

'I DON'T UNDERSTAND YOU.'

They were the words he awoke to the next morning. He stared at the face that belonged on his pillow.

'Where did the other earring come from?' Luka asked, because she was wearing both.

'I always carry it in my purse,' Sophie said.

She would carry her mother with her for ever, Luka knew. If the truth was ever revealed she would never forgive and he was right not to trust her with his heart.

Some things were too big to come back from.

'You don't understand me, Sophie, because I won't let you.'

He rose from the bed.

'Will you let me try?'

It was the calmest they had ever been, like

sweeping up the debris after a wild party that neither regretted.

'No,' Luka said. 'Sophie...' He sat on the bed and took her hand. 'We had a love that most people never know. You know that saying...better to have loved and lost—'

'I *hate* that saying,' Sophie broke in. 'I hate that saying more than any other. Who wrote that?' Sophie demanded.

'Tennyson.'

'Well, he was wrong.'

'I agree,' Luka said. 'I wish I'd never loved you.'

'But you did.'

'I did.'

'And you don't now?'

Luka wasn't that good a liar so he gave her a kiss instead. A nice one, not a loaded one. A sweet one, if, between them there could be such a thing.

'In a few days this will be over,' Luka said. 'We're going to get back to our lives knowing that we did the right thing by your father. It will be easier on us both once we get to Bordo Del Cielo.'

'How?'

'I'll check into the hotel and, like a good groom, I'll stay well away from the blushing bride-to-be.'

'Not as blushing as I'll be when you jilt me.'

'I can't marry you, Sophie. I can't be your fake husband. I can't stand in a church and exchange vows that I know we can't keep.'

He got up and headed to the bathroom.

'Hey, Luka,' Sophie said. 'I wished I'd never loved you too.'

The calm did not just belong in the bedroom.

A new presence had arrived with the dawn, though no one fully acknowledged it.

The colour seemed to have drained from Paulo's irises, Luka noticed as he wished him good morning.

And as Sophie passed her father his coffee and his shaking hand reached for it, it was a natural transition for her to lift the cup to his lips and help him to drink it.

The nurse stood, about to help, but Sophie shook her head.

'I've got this.'

So too had Luka.

He was so kind to Paulo and so engaged in organising the quick wedding that there were times Sophie had to catch herself because it felt real.

'What about the evening?' Paulo wheezed.

'The hotel is already holding a function,' Sophie explained, and she looked at Luka, but he shook his head. There was nothing he could do. It had been the first thing he had sold. 'The hotel is under new ownership.'

'We don't need that hotel,' Paulo said. 'Before it was built we would party in the street. I remember my wedding to your mother—we came out of the church and straight into a feast. Perhaps you could ring Teresa at the deli and see if she can sort out the food and the drinks...'

'Pa...' Sophie looked over to where her father sat. 'Why would Teresa want to help us when you—?'

'Sophie.' Luka stopped her from continuing and then watched as Sophie walked out onto the balcony. He could see her hands gripping the railing as she fought not to confront her father. Despite Paulo insisting he wasn't confused, he seemed to live between the long-ago past—when Rosa had been alive—and then the present, as if he had simply erased the damage that had been caused in between.

'*Scusi*,' Luka said to Paulo, and walked out to join her.

'He gets confused,' Luka said patiently.

'He gets confused when it suits him.'

'No,' Luka said. 'I don't think he can reconcile what he has done. He needs to go home. I can see that now.'

'No one will be talking to him, though,' Sophie said. 'Have you asked Matteo to be your groomsman?'

'I have.'

'And what did he say?'

'That he'll move things around so that he can be there.'

'I want Bella there too.'

'I'm not sure if that's wise,' Luka said. 'Matteo will be with Shandy. You know a bit of what went down between him and Bella.'

'I believe that it was Bella who went down,' Sophie said. 'And your friend paid for the pleasure.'

'You don't let a single thing go.'

'You refused my offer of a clean slate,' Sophie pointed out. 'So tell your friend that, however uncomfortable Bella's presence might make him, she'll be there.' She rubbed her temples and dragged in air. 'I need to sort out some accommodation for us.'

'That's all sorted,' Luka said.

'How?'

'Come on.' Luka led her back inside then he addressed her father. 'Paulo,' he said in a very practical voice, 'you will be tired after the ceremony. Perhaps we could have a few people back to your home…'

He gave a pale smile as Sophie let herself back in but then Paulo spoke. 'I don't have a home there any more.'

'Yes, Paulo,' Luka said, 'you do. Since his death my lawyers have been sorting out the properties that my father acquired. You have your home to return to. It is all there, nothing has been changed. Angela has been taking care of it.'

For this gift to her father Sophie could almost forgive Luka for not loving her enough to remain in her life.

'I have a home,' Paulo sobbed. 'Your mother's dress will be there, Sophie. You can wear it for the wedding.'

'No!' It was Sophie who interrupted Paulo. 'I'm not wearing my mother's dress. I'm not my mother...'

'Sophie, please,' her father begged, but on this she stood firm.

'I don't want a replica of your marriage, Pa.' She was caught between the truth and a lie. 'I want our marriage to be different.'

She was torn, completely, as she walked out of the lounge and into the bedroom.

'What was all that about?' Luka asked, having followed her in. 'I thought you were trying to give him the wedding of his dreams before he dies.'

'Remember that you said if this was real, if we were in love...?' Sophie turned the tables on him. 'Then my father would know I would not be simply agreeing to everything. My father sees those times through rose-coloured glasses. If we really were marrying...'

'Go on.'

'What's the point in going on?' Sophie demanded. 'Why should I tell you the wife and woman I want to be when you're not even prepared to be there to find out? Why should I trust you with my dreams again when you won't let me into your heart? You can have sex with me. Luka, you can be kind to me, you can argue with me if you must, but don't ask for my private thoughts when we both know that you're planning to walk away from me.' She couldn't continue speaking. 'I'm going to Bella's.'

'We need to get organised for tomorrow.'

'I am organised,' Sophie said. 'We have the church booked, we have your plane to take us. I'll call Teresa and then I'm going out.'

It was amongst the hardest of calls she had ever

made. Teresa was as cold and as hesitant as before, but, Sophie guessed, work was work for her and perhaps it was because of the mention of the Cavaliere name that Teresa agreed to cater back at the house for the wedding.

'*Grazie,*' Sophie said, and hung up.

She collected her bag from the bedroom and gave her father a kiss on the cheek.

'How long will you be?' Paulo asked.

'You'll be in bed by the time I'm back.' Sophie smiled. 'I'll see you in the morning. Just think, Pa, this time tomorrow you'll be back in Bordo Del Cielo. You can sleep well tonight, dreaming of that. I love you so much.'

It was getting harder and harder to say goodnight, never knowing if this would be the last time.

She went over and gave Luka the necessary kiss. 'Soon,' Sophie said, as she lowered her head and kissed his mouth then whispered into his ear, 'we'll be living apart…'

'What time will you be back?' Luka asked.

'You're not my husband yet.' Sophie smiled

with her lips but not with her eyes and then she moved her mouth to his ear. 'Dawn,' she whispered, 'so, as said, you can sleep well.'

She could not stand another night spent next to a man she could never have so she headed to the door, but Luka followed her out.

'The plane leaves at seven.'

'I'll be back well before then.'

'Tonight might be our last chance to talk...'

'What's the point?' Sophie said. 'There's nothing left to say. We both know what you're going to do to me. You're wrong, Luka, I'm not fourteen, you don't have to prise me from you knee. I'll be at the church, and if you're not...' Sophie shrugged. 'I'll survive. I've had an awful lot of practice.'

She held it together until she made it to the apartment and only there, with Bella, did she finally let her guard down.

'He says he wishes he'd never loved me.'

'At least you have known love... Better to have—'

'Don't,' Sophie warned. 'If you start quoting Tennyson, I'll scream!

'Who's Tennyson?'

'I don't really know,' Sophie said, 'but I don't think he understood the heart...'

But maybe he did, because the thought of never having known Luka's love filled her with dread.

'He's going to jilt me.'

'More fool him,' Bella said.

'And I had a bit of an argument with my father. He wants me to wear my mother's wedding dress and I said no. I don't want a marriage like theirs.'

'I'm already making your dress,' Bella said. 'I guessed that this might happen when Luka agreed to get engaged so I've already started it. I kept some money back from our savings and I bought some chiffon from the market. I will work on it through the night.'

'I'm going to be there with you, Sophie.'

'No.' Sophie shook her head because despite her brave words to Luka she could not put her friend through that. 'You have to work, and anyway...'

'Anyway?'

'Matteo will be there and...' Sophie could hardly bear to tell her, but Bella already knew.

'I know that he has a woman,' Bella said. 'And I know that she's stunning. I'd love to come and be your bridesmaid, Sophie. And don't worry about work—as of this morning I am suspended.'

'Bella?'

'I got in a lot of trouble,' Bella said. 'I spilt an ice bucket on a guest's lap when I was delivering the breakfasts to the room.'

'An ice bucket.'

'It was mainly cold water. I tripped but his girlfriend kicked up a fuss and called for the manager. It was a simple accident. The room was dark. I didn't see him—or rather they didn't hear me come in with breakfast... They were otherwise engaged.'

Sophie looked up to the sound of venom and mischief in Bella's voice and her mouth actually gaped for a moment before speaking.

'You threw a bucket of iced water over Matteo?'

'I did.' Bella grinned. 'So, you see, now I am free to be at your wedding and I'm going to make your the wedding dress. Sophie, you're going to be the most beautiful bride.'

'Even if he doesn't get to see me?'

'Oh, he'll see you,' Bella said. 'I'll make sure Matteo takes a few pictures as you arrive.' She hugged her friend and recited a Siclian saying. *'"Di guerra, caccia e amuri, pri un gustu milli duluri."'*

In war, hunting and love you suffer a thousand pains for one pleasure.

'The pleasure will be yours,' Bella said.

'It won't be, though,' Sophie said.

She was tired of the old ways, tired of false pride and sayings that spoke of revenge.

She was tired, so tired of hollow victories.

Maybe she had grown up.

Sophie wanted the man she loved.

CHAPTER SIXTEEN

SOPHIE'S FLIGHT BACK to Bordo Del Cielo was very different from the one she had taken when she had left.

Then she had been nineteen—confused, hurting, angry and just so glad to be getting away.

Now she was confused but the hurt was different.

Paulo was asleep in the bedroom area; Bella was sitting in one of the luxurious chairs with a curtain around her because she didn't want anyone to see the dress she was making for her friend.

Sophie sat beside Luka, staring out of the window and watching the land she wanted to love but which had cost her so much come into view.

'I was wrong,' Luka said, and she turned.

'Oh, you are so wrong,' Sophie said. No doubt

he was talking about something else but all she knew was that he was wrong not to give them this chance.

Luka gave a soft, wry laugh as if he knew what she was thinking. 'I thought you were lying when you said that you were an events planner but I know few women who could organise a wedding in a couple of days.'

'It's easy to when you know...' Sophie shrugged. 'Well, let's just say I'm not too worried about how the cake is going to look and whether Teresa has had enough notice.' She looked right into his eyes. 'How could you even consider doing this to him, Luka?'

'How could you have done this to us?'

His words didn't confuse her, they ate at her instead.

She remembered standing on the beach, confused and ashamed and shouting, when their mouths should have been kissing.

She remembered hurling the sins of his father at him when she should have loved him first.

The plane came in to land and they sat in silence, but as they hit the tarmac, as they hurtled down the runway, Sophie didn't care if the plane lifted now and took them away.

But it came to a halt and they were home.

'I'm not perfect...' Sophie turned to him '... but I'd fight for us.'

'Nice speech,' Luka said. 'Tell me, though, Sophie—when did you ever fight for us? Did you come to my father's funeral? You would have known I had no one, the hell it would be to come home...'

'I was going to,' Sophie said, 'but I had just found out that my father was terminally ill.'

'He still is,' Luka replied, unmoved. 'You've held up the death card and I'm here. That's not an excuse not to show up on the day you would have known I needed you the most.'

He accepted no excuses for her carelessness with their love.

Did she sit there now and tell him the truth?

That he was right?

It hadn't been her father's illness that had stopped her contacting him.

Did she tell him she couldn't have afforded it?

Would a man like Luka accept as an excuse that she'd had no money? That he'd have had to wire her the fare?

'Did you fight for us on the beach, when I pleaded with you to come with me?' Luka asked.

'No.'

Her single word moved him. She did not kick up with her usual defence as to how he had shamed her in court.

'So when did you fight for us, Sophie?'

'I'll fight now.'

Luka said nothing.

He just stood as the passengers disembarked.

'I'll see you to your home,' Luka said.

It was a strange ride.

Her father never stopped coughing. There was the angel of death in the car with them and turned backs on the streets as Sophie looked out.

Yet it was home.

And it was somehow beautiful.

'Do you remember...?' She stopped.

Eight years old to his fourteen, she had found

Luka crying for the first and last time, washing blood from his face in the river.

'Did you fall?' she had asked.

'Yes, I fell.'

They had sat eating nectarines and she had looked at his bruised, bloodied nose and closed eye.

'One day,' Sophie had said, 'you will be taller than him.'

'Who?' Luka had asked, because then he had still been loyal to his father.

'Taller than any man in this town,' she had said.

'I remember,' Luka said, and she did not turn or jump to the sound of his voice.

Here it felt normal.

Here they were as entwined as the vines and the roots beneath them.

They passed the school where she had left at fifteen to work in the hotel.

'I cried the day I left,' Sophie admitted. 'I wanted to learn all the poems. I wanted to sort out the maths...'

'You have the cleverest head on the planet,' Luka said.

'Yet I can't work us out.'

'We're here,' Bella said, and Sophie looked as they turned from the hotel and into her street.

It was the same, except different.

The neighbour's house had changed and was *tastefully* renovated. 'It smells of London.' Sophie winked as she waved to her weekender neighbours.

'I'll leave you here,' Luka said, having helped Paulo up the path.

'You're not going to come in for coffee?'

'I'm going to go and check into the hotel,' Luka said, once he had ensured everything was okay. 'And then I am meeting with Matteo.'

He didn't want to go in.

He didn't want to see just how poor his father had kept them.

'I might go for a walk,' Bella said. 'I would like to look at my old home, even if there are other people living there...'

Sophie looked at Luka but he gave her a slight

shake of his head and pulled her aside. 'I haven't told everyone what I am doing. I don't want anyone feeling beholden. My lawyer will contact people once I've gone. Bella will find out soon enough that she has a home.'

Thank God for the nurse, because she took an exhausted, overwrought Paulo to his room for some oxygen and medication.

'It is your last day as a single woman,' Paulo wheezed. 'You should go out with Bella.'

'I'm just happy to be home.'

Sophie was. Though it felt so strange to be back.

Happy her father was settled, she set to work. There was a lot to be done and also there was Teresa to pay.

She walked into town, trying not to look up. She didn't want to see Malvolio's home spreading out over the top of the hill.

She didn't want to glimpse the bedroom where she and Luka had first made love and she averted her eyes as she passed the church where tomorrow he would leave her standing.

Sophie walked into Teresa's deli and, just as they had the last time she'd done so, the people in the deli fell silent. Angela was there, chatting with Teresa and a couple of other locals, and Sophie felt her cheeks turn to fire as she stepped up to the counter.

'I've come to pay for the catering for the wedding tomorrow.'

'*Gratuitamente*,' Teresa said, and Sophie was about to slam the money down, as she had all those years ago, but she chose not to.

She was older and wiser now, even if she'd prefer not to be at times.

'Teresa, I know it must be difficult for you to know that my father is back. He just wants to see Luka and I marry...' Just as Sophie always did, she held back her tears. 'That is all we are here for, to give my father some peace in his final days. Soon we'll be gone and out of your lives for good.'

'Sophie?' Angela asked. 'How is Paulo?'

'He's weak. He just wants to be home and to see me married.' She put down the money. 'We don't want any trouble.'

She walked out of the deli. A part of Sophie wanted to go to the beach, to sit there a while and remember days when life had seemed so much simpler, but instead she made her way home.

Bella was back from her walk and busy finishing off the dress, and Sophie dealt with the flowers and cleaning the house, as she had done so many times before. But then Paulo awoke and declared that he wanted to visit his wife's grave.

It was a long slow walk to the hill.

And agony to walk back down.

Spare me from your grief, she wanted to plead to her father as the nurse took him, weeping, to bed.

'Another walk?' Sophie smiled as Bella again headed out with a full face of make-up.

'Who knows who I might bump into?' Bella smiled.

Almost the moment she left there was a knock at the door and, no, it wasn't Bella to recheck her make-up, it was the priest.

'Do you want to let your father know I am here?'

Sophie nodded.

He looked so tired when she went into his room and Sophie knew then that tomorrow might not be the embarrassment she was dreading. Luka had been right. The journey, no matter how luxurious, had depleted him and visiting Rosa seemed to have taken the last of his strength.

'The priest is here,' Sophie said. 'Do you want me to send him through?'

'Please.'

She went out to the garden and lay on a sun lounger and tried not to think of what was happening. Her heart seemed to still as she felt a shadow fall over her and she looked up into the strained features of Luka.

'You're crying.'

'No,' Sophie corrected, 'because I never cry. I don't think I know how to. I'm just tired.' She looked up into navy eyes. 'The priest is in with my father. He is making his confession. I would expect him to be some considerable time.'

He sat down by her knees on the sun lounger but she shrank away.

'Please, don't be a hypocrite,' Sophie said. 'Don't offer me your arms and then remove them tomorrow. I'm drained, Luka. I'm tired of being a parent to my father. I'm exhausted from absorbing his tears so I'm going to sit and watch the sunset and then I'll get up and put on my green dress, as per tradition, for a Sicilian bride on the eve of her wedding.'

'About tomorrow—'

'I'm not even thinking about tomorrow, Luka,' she interrupted. 'The day will bring what it shall bring and I'll survive it.' She looked up as the priest came out and stood to see him out.

'He's made his confession.'

Luka heard the priest's reedy voice as Sophie saw him out.

It was, Luka knew, time for him to make his confession.

Just not to Sophie.

Paulo was sitting in bed, holding his rosary beads and a picture of Rosa, but he turned and smiled as Luka made his way over and joined him.

'Is it good to be home?' Luka asked.

'It is,' Paulo said. 'I have made my confessions. Most of them anyway.' He looked at Luka. 'How long will you two pretend to be together for? Till after my funeral?'

'What are you talking about, Paulo?'

'I'm not a fool. I've always known that Sophie was lying to me. I knew, with what you said about her in court, that you were over before you even started.'

'She doesn't forgive easily.'

'She is like Rosa.' Paulo smiled. 'Even if I believed at first you were together, we do see the news in prison. I've read about your affairs and your scandals. I've seen the many beautiful women that you've dated.'

'You went along with it?' Luka frowned as he sat on the edge of the bed.

'She thought it made me happy knowing she was being taken care of.'

'Yet here you are you are. pushing for us to get married, even though you know it is a ruse. Why?'

'Because for all the mistakes I have made in my life, that wasn't one of them. You two are right for each other. I hoped that maybe being forced to spend time together you both might see that. It didn't work though.'

'No,' Luka admitted.

'It's time to be honest,' Paulo said. 'Now, while we still have time to be.'

Luka gave a small nod.

'You paid people a lot of money to work on my case these past months. What happened to make you suddenly want my release?'

'I always thought you were weak,' Luka admitted. 'I saw you as my father's yes-man but then I found something and I realised then that you had been protecting the person you love most.' He went into his pocket and handed Paulo the cross and chain. 'I found this amongst my father's things.'

Paulo let out a small cry as he took his beloved wife's cross and chain and pressed it to his lips.

'You knew her death was my father's doing, didn't you?'

'Not at first but eventually I did,' Paulo said. 'Malvolio wanted to build the hotel on the foreshore but there were families, including Rosa and I, who did not want to sell our homes.' He took a moment to take some long breaths from his oxygen mask and then continued speaking. 'I said to Rosa that we should move away and just leave Boro Del Cielo but she would not be run out of town—she said that someone had to stand up to him.' It was the most difficult conversation. With every sentence Paulo paused to breathe. 'Rosa went to see him to give him a piece of her mind. A few days later there was a car accident. I didn't connect the two at first. I was grieving and Malvolio was the white knight, the friend...' He started to cough.

'Enough,' Luka said.

'No.' Paulo was insistent that he finish. 'He said to put differences aside—he organised the funeral when I could not. He spoke at the service when I had no words. When I told him that I could not stand to be in the home we had loved he moved me here...' Paulo looked around at what had been his and Sophie's home. 'It took a few months for me to come out of the fog and start to see what had happened. He had got us out of our home by any means. By then I knew what he was capable of. He never threatened that harm would come to Sophie—instead, he said how lucky she was that he would look out for her, that our children would one day marry.'

'But the implication was there?' Luka asked, and Paulo nodded.

'When did you know?' Paulo asked.

'About Rosa?' Luka checked. 'When I found her necklace amongst my father's things, although I knew that he was corrupt long before that. It's the reason I rarely came home.'

'You came home that day to end things with Sophie?'

'I did,' Luka said. 'I just wanted to break all ties with this place. It wasn't that easy, though.'

'Love never is,' Paulo said, and held out the chain to Luka.

'Why are you giving this to me?' Luka asked.

'I would have liked to be buried holding it,'

Paulo admitted, but then he shook his head. 'If I was then Sophie would have to know what had happened.' Paulo spoke his absolute truth. 'She would never forgive you, Luka. I know my daughter and the fact that your family was involved in her mother's death is something that she would not be able to forgive. Take the necklace and throw it the ocean when I am gone,' Paulo said. 'I will take your secret to the grave.'

'It's not my secret,' Luka said.

'It can be,' Paulo said. 'Sophie loves you and you love her. You do not need this hanging over you. Please.' He gave the cross and chain one final kiss and handed it back to Luka. 'Never tell her the truth. There is no need.'

Luka pocketed the chain and walked out from the bedroom to the lounge. There was Sophie and she gave him a tired smile.

'How is he?'

'He's okay.'

'You?'

Luka didn't answer. There was lie in his pocket and he didn't know how to handle it. Her own father had told him that their love could not survive it, but as he went to walk off Sophie halted him.

'I was wrong, Luka. I should have come to London with you that night.'

'Why?'

'I just should have. I was angry and I blamed you.'

'When did you decide this?'

'Just now.'

'Five years after the event,' Luka sneered. His emotions were everywhere. 'You let it fester for five years.'

'Luka...'

'So what happens when the shoe drops, Sophie? What happens when the next bombshell hits? Am I to wait another five years for you to come around? Am I to wait again for you to swallow that Sicilian pride?'

'You refuse to give me that chance.'

'I do.'

CHAPTER SEVENTEEN

'REMEMBER HOW WE used to sit here?' Bella said, as they sat bathed in sunrise with their calves dangling in cool water.

'I do.' Sophie smiled. 'I also remember the terrible row I had here with Luka.'

'It is a glorious day for a wedding.'

'A wedding that isn't going to happen,' Sophie said.

'He loves you,' Bella said. 'I can see it in him. Luka would not leave you standing in the church. He would not have come to Sicily just to shame you.'

'He told me he would never go through with it. Is it wrong that I wish my father would die before three p.m., just to spare him the shame?'

'I think so.' Bella smiled.

'Luka is as stubborn as I am.' Sophie sighed.

'He accuses me of being Sicilian as he trips on his own pride. I'm going to be jilted.'

'You could always have a fall this morning.' Bella smiled again. 'Slip on one of those rocks up there...'

'I could,' Sophie said. 'Or I could get a cramp, swimming, and you have to save me but I swallowed so much sea water that I was too weak to make it to the church...'

They laughed, they sat at the water's edge and laughed, and it felt so good to do so.

'Let him jilt me,' Sophie said. 'Let's really give the people of Bordo Del Cielo some scandal again. The girls are back in town!'

'Sisters in shame,' Bella said.

Sophie looked at her dear friend, who was terrified about today too.

'Are you scared to face Matteo?'

'I'm ashamed to face him.'

'He paid for a night with you, remember. You wouldn't be a whore if it wasn't for his money.'

'I know,' Bella said. 'If he tries anything I will tell him he can't afford me now!'

They laughed again and then Bella stood. 'Come on, we have a lot to do today.'

'You go back,' Sophie said. 'I might just sit here a while.'

'I will give your pa breakfast.'

'Thank you.'

Alone she sat and stared out at the water and at the cargo ships and cruise liners so far out on the horizon.

Out of reach for ever.

She was going to cry.

It hit her as surely as the sensation that she might vomit.

It felt like thunder rising in her chest and, like a cat hiding, she moved to the shelter of the cliffs and curled into her knees and wept.

For the father she would soon lose.

For the future devoid of Luka.

But most of all for the love she *had* known.

A love that could never be replicated or surpassed. She was exhausted, not just from the past but already from a future without him. How she loathed the poets she did not understand, but even with a lifetime to study them she wanted one that matched her, that told her how to deal with a future without Luka in it.

'You're going to startle,' Luka said. 'As you do every time I approach.'

'Well, I've never had the chance to get used to the sound of your voice,' she said, and wiped her eyes and looked up. 'So, yes, every time we meet in the future, expect me to jump. How did you know I was here?'

'Bella told me. She is sitting in the morning sun with your father. Matteo and I met her walking back...'

'Walking back from what? Your stag night?'

'There are no bucks' nights in Sicily,' Luka said. 'We did our best, though. We drank at the hotel till it closed and then walked along the shore.'

'You should go,' Sophie said. 'It's bad luck to see me on the morning of the wedding.'

'We've had our share of bad luck,' he said. 'How is your father this morning?' he asked, and this time she didn't accuse him of not caring.

She knew that he did.

'He will live to see his daughter jilted.'

Luka sat down beside her.

Paulo would know why he could not go through with the wedding. It should not be her father who would have to explain things to Sophie. It was for that reason he sat down to tell her, and braced himself for the most difficult conversation of his life.

'Why do you hate me, Luka?'

'As I said before, there are many reasons.' It should be odd that he took her hand to break her heart, but to Sophie it wasn't. 'Remember the night we parted? How angry you were, how you refused to give me a chance to explain? How you compared me to my father?'

'I was nineteen years old then.'

'No, Sophie, that's my excuse when I go over that time,' Luka said. 'I was younger, I was just out of prison, I had no idea what was going on. I had said things in court that I regretted, things I know I would handle better if they happened today. I'd run rings around that barrister now.'

'I know that you would.'

'I've changed,' Luka said. 'You haven't.'

'You mean I'm not sophisticated enough for you?'

'I mean your fire remains.' He snapped his fingers in front of her eyes. '*That* is how long it takes for you to make up your mind, Sophie— you decide things in an instant and nothing will change your mind.'

It was true, Sophie knew, for almost the second he had opened the door to her she had fallen in love and nothing had dimmed that.

'Almost nothing changes my mind,' Sophie refuted. 'I regret the words I said. I was confused, I was hurting…'

'I know that,' Luka said. 'How long did it take for you to see things from my side? To calm down?'

'I don't know.'

'Nearly five years,' Luka said. 'It has taken you until we are on our knees, till we are all but over, for you to see things from my side.'

'No, I knew almost straight away.'

'What did you do about it?' Luka challenged. 'Did you try to look me up in London? Did you do anything to let me know that you were wrong?'

'No.'

'Only now will you admit that you can see things from my side, that you were wrong.'

'Are you saying that I have to be perfect?'

'No,' Luka said, 'I love your stubbornness. You would argue the sky was purple. I love your fire and that you are pure Sicilian yet it is what will ultimately tear us apart.'

'I don't understand,' she said. 'Is it because I lied?'

'Tell me your lies,' Luka said. 'Let's do this once and for all. Tell me your lies and secrets and I'll tell you mine.'

'Why?'

'Because the truth can't hurt us any more than this does.'

'I'm poor,' Sophie said. 'Bella and I are as poor as church mice and we fooled you with my wardrobe and phone.'

Luka just smiled.

'You knew that?'

'Not really. Though I did wonder about you being an events manager,' Luka admitted.

'I'm a chambermaid.'

'You were when I met you.'

She loathed that she hadn't moved on but he melted that fear with four words. 'I loved you then.'

'You don't care?'

'I don't care about money and things. I admit that I like not having to worry about it and, yes, I like nice things but, at the end of day, if it all falls into the ocean I would survive without it. My father had more money that a team of accountants can trace and yet he was the poorest man I have ever known.'

'I'm sorry.'

'For what?'

'For not being there for his funeral.'

'It doesn't matter.'

'It does. My father has done a lot of things wrong but I still love him.'

'My father did worse.'

'The hurt is more, then,' Sophie said. 'I don't think you can ever remove love. Even when by others' standards it deserves to be removed, even by your own... Love is not a whiteboard, Luka, it doesn't come with an eraser.'

'I can't make a good man out of him,' Luka said, 'but there were times when my mother was still alive that I remember with some affection. After that...' He shook his head. 'So what are your other lies?

'I feel like I trapped you that day we first made love. That you didn't see the real me. I am the peasant you despise. When you opened the door I was dressed in my finest with my mother's earrings, some make-up that I was trying out for our engagement, the dress...'

'Sophie, I hate that I said that to my father about you. I can't take it back, just explain that it was a row between him and I. It should never have been replayed in court. As to trapping me, well, I spent six months in prison, and within that time I spent two very long months alone when I thought about that day a lot... Do you think, when I replayed that time, I recalled that you were wearing your mother's earrings?'

He moved his head and he kissed the lobe of her ear, kissed it with such tenderness that it was as if it was the most important layer of skin that had ever existed. 'Do you think,' he asked, 'when I touch you that I remember the make-up?' His mouth moved to her eyelids and again he was so gentle and Sophie started crying because she knew, she just knew that right here, right now, he was kissing her goodbye; she just didn't understand why. 'I promise you, Sophie,' he said, his mouth moving down her neck, 'when I recalled that time, not once did I think of the dress you were wearing. I thought of these...'

He slipped the knot from her top and her breasts were naked to the morning sun and to his mouth.

'When I go over that time,' Luka said, and his fingers moved up her dress and to the silk of her panties, which were damp as he slid them down. She moaned as his fingers slipped into her. 'I remember you naked... I remember taking you for the first time, and the noises you made.'

He pushed her slowly down and onto her back. It was Sophie who slipped off her panties as Luka unzipped. Half-dressed but naked to the very soul, she stared into his eyes.

'When I come, every time I remember this...'

He seared inside her, and his face was over hers, and Sophie didn't try to hold back the tears as together they revisited that day.

'I remember you coming. I remember how I tried so hard not to.'

He moved up on his elbows and looked down at her. 'I don't want to come because when I do...'

'You're going to leave me, aren't you?'

How could he be making love to her while nodding that, yes, they were over?

She had lived in the moment just once in her life. That afternoon when the dog had ceased barking, when the surroundings had faded, Sophie had glimpsed the present, and she found it again now.

The past slipped away and the future was unseen, and she kissed the man she loved. She kissed his mouth and his rough cheek, she kissed the scar she had closed and, try as she might not to just yet, she started to come to him.

'Don't,' Sophie begged, because once Luka came it was over, but his tide was coming in.

She knew from the only body she truly knew—his.

His moan was one of pain as he released because it signalled the end, but even in the last throes Sophie might have lost her heart but her head remained and she looked into his navy eyes as he offered her one last chance.

"Will you fight for us?' Luka asked.

He pulled out, he dressed and then he dressed her and he asked her again. 'Now, with what I have to tell you, will you fight for us as you promised?' He went on, 'Will your words still be kind and wise when we face a test?' He placed a gram of gold in her hand and it felt like a weighted ball, with no burden lifted, as he handed it over to her.

'I found it when my father died. I came back to Bordo for the funeral and I was going through my father's things.'

'Your father did this... You...' She halted,

tripped over her words. She tried to remember she was fighting for them but she was breathless on the ropes in her mother's corner.

'You see, Sophie, with this you can win every row. You can take the shame of what my father did and give it to me over and over. But I can't live like that. The reason I will never marry you is this—I have lied under oath to protect your family. It didn't work. I have lied on the Bible, I have attempted over and over to edit the truth. No more. I will not stand in a church and lie and take you as a temporary wife when the truth is I will love you for ever.'

Anger, rage, fury, hissed at an unknown target.

'I don't care if you're poor. I don't care if you have lied, cheated...whatever...' Luka continued. 'You do what you have to to survive but I know my limits, Sophie. I know I love you. I accept you but I cannot compromise with this. I cannot take more of his shame. I cannot say sorry any more for a person I am not. Know that.

'I love you,' Luka said. 'I love the life we could have, but I care about myself too. I have dreams and ambitions and I will never be brought to my knees again for that man.'

'Luka, how long have you known?'

'When he died.'

'And you never guessed before then?'

This was her mother who had died—*her mother*!

'I need to know. How long have you had your suspicions?'

'I can remember your mother coming to our house. She was angry at my father for trying to get them out of their home. Your father had warned her they should leave yet she refused...' Luka tried to look with adult eyes at a child's past and then he lost his cool.

'I won't let you do this to us, Sophie,' he shouted. 'You want facts? I found out for sure a year ago. I have known for a lifetime he was rotten to the core. If you want a dissection then get a dead frog—they don't bleed and anyway their blood is already cold. Mine's warm. My heart beats. I won't let you do it to me.'

She came out fighting then.

Sophie pushed herself off the ropes that bound her and entered the ring.

For them.

'You criticise me for comparing you to your father, yet over and over you compare me to my mother. Not just you,' Sophie said, 'but my father, the whole town does. "She is like Rosa..."' The only sound was silence. 'I am like her, just as you are like your father. But you are not him. You are arrogant, you are clever and you are strong, but you are good. I am fierce, I have a temper, but I would listen when the man I love told me that we had to leave. Did I march to your father and demand Bella's freedom of choice?' Sophie shouted. 'No. I offered to and when she said no, when she said she must stay, I respected her choice...as I have to respect that you can't marry me.'

'I can never be your fake husband, Sophie.'

She looked at him.

'Can we get past this?'

'I don't know,' she admitted. Questions were swirling, dates and times and anger and blame, and Luka smiled at her honest answer.

'You get to decide, Sophie. I'll be there today. Jilt *me* if you think I deserve it for what he did. Score your point for your fleeting victory but I win because I know you will regret it for ever if you don't show up today. No one ever shall, or ever could, love you as much as I do.'

'You love me so much that you invite me to end us—?'

'I love you so much,' Luka interrupted, 'that I won't relegate us to a poor future. I would rather have sex with a stranger for the rest of my life than lie next to you cold and blaming. I would rather have half a marriage, half a life, half of me, if I cannot have all of you. For you to deny me that part of you…for you to hold me hostage…' He shook his proud head. 'Fight with me about things if you want to, be every inch Sicilian. Call me on what my father did once. I might get that, but if you call me on it twice…'

And Luka dared accuse *her* of being Sicilian!

'I don't give second warnings,' Luka said. 'My father was responsible for the death of your mother. I will not let his sins, or your anger, bring me to my knees. If you walk into that church,' Luka warned, 'then you'd better know that it's for ever. You only walk towards me if you can love me more than the shadows of our past. If you can't, then it is better for both of us that you walk away.'

Luka did the nicest thing then.

Her breast was precariously close to falling out again so he redid the tie to her halter-neck and re-arranged her dress. He looked after her in a way that no one ever could and he demanded that she match that care.

Always.

'Show up or don't,' Luka said. 'Hate me at your own peril.'

'What will you do if I don't turn up?'

'Nothing,' Luka said. And it was, for Sophie, the darkest response he could deliver. 'If you don't show for our wedding then nothing will happen, not ever. I will wish you luck for the future, I will accept that our love could not survive. I'll be proud of you for having the guts to admit it and,' he added, 'I will get on with my life.'

He left her on the rocks.
He left her spinning like a Catherine wheel.
There was a retort she could deliver.
A proud last word, perhaps.
There was comeuppance still to be had.
Or there was a shiny new future?

CHAPTER EIGHTEEN

'YOU LOOK WONDERFUL,' Bella said.

It was possibly the most beautiful dress in the world and might, Sophie knew, remain unseen.

He had left her with seven hours to grow up.

She was down to twelve minutes.

'Are you scared he won't show up?'

It was no longer a town of secrets but what had happened on the beach Sophie had kept to herself.

This was between her and Luka.

She was scared that *she* might not. Scared that her rapid tongue could not hold its fire.

Sophie pulled out the necklace.

I love you, she said in her head to her mother. *I come from you but I am not you.*

'It looks like the one in the photos that your

mother wore,' Bella said, as she helped her to put it on.

'It is the one my mother wore,' Sophie said, and she felt Bella's hands pause on her naked shoulders.

Bella knew, Sophie realised.

Here there were secrets even amongst the very closest of friends.

Her mother would probably have known and would have told Bella the truth long ago. The whole town would have been able to see what a small child could not.

Rosa had gone and confronted Malvolio.

A few days later she had died.

'Why didn't my father insist that they run?' Sophie asked. She knew the answer—Rosa, with her stubbornness and pride, had been right to want to stay.

Dead right.

'Can you ever forgive him?'

'Malvolio?' Sophie scoffed. 'Never.'

'I mean can you ever fully forgive Luka for what Malvolio did?' Bella asked, but hushed as Paulo walked in.

'Their names don't belong in the same breath,' Paulo said, his eyes filling with tears when he saw that Sophie was wearing Rosa's chain.

'But they do belong in the same breath,' Sophie corrected. 'Just as I belong in the same breath as my mother. Just as I look like her and act like her at times. I'm not her, though.'

'I know that.'

'Even if she's not here, I've learnt from her…'

'The cars are here,' Bella said.

'Go,' Sophie said to Bella. 'I will see you at the church.' She gave her friend a hug. 'Good luck with Matteo.'

She stood alone with her father.

'You are your mother's daughter. That is not always a compliment. I wanted to leave here, to get away. She told me to stand up to him, to fight for what was right.' Sophie stood as her father shook his head. 'So I did. I had our tickets booked to leave. I wanted to get out of here…'

'You were right.'

'I would rather have been wrong.'

'Malvolio *is* Luka's father,' Sophie said. 'At

times they will belong in the same breath. I don't want a marriage where there are things that cannot be discussed or names that can never be mentioned. I nearly lost Luka, not once but twice. I am not going to do that again. I shan't make the same mistakes as...'

'Me?'

'As so many people did,' Sophie said, more aware than ever how words could hurt so very much. 'You did the best that you could for me. I know that.'

'Not really.'

'Yes, really.' Sophie smiled at her father. 'You got one thing very right—you chose the perfect husband for me.'

'You and Luka belong to each other.'

'We do.'

It wasn't just the bride who was nervous on a wedding day, Luka was finding out.

The groom stood at the altar when, for the longest time, he had thought that he never would.

Luka had long ago accepted that he and Sophie were over and, given that he had known he would never love like that again, he had decided he would remain single.

Until this morning.

This morning he had chosen for their sakes to take the biggest gamble of his life and to reveal the truth.

Her own father thought that Sophie could never forgive him and Matteo too was tense.

And so he stood on his wedding day not even knowing if Sophie would show up.

He didn't care about the public reaction if the bride didn't show.

He cared only about them.

'Whatever happens—' Matteo started, but Luka halted him.

'She'll be here.'

He had confidence in them, in the love they had found that long-ago afternoon.

And he was right to.

He turned around and there was Sophie, dressed in a simple white dress that reminded him of yesteryear. Today her black hair was worn down, as he preferred, and dotted with summer jasmine. In one hand she loosely held a bunch of wild Sicilian poppies and they were as sexy and as decadent and as heady as her.

The delighted, stunned look on her face when she saw the packed church was something he would remember for ever.

They loved her and understood too just how hard it had been for Paulo.

He was home, where he belonged, and ready now for his daughter to leave properly.

She walked towards him and Luka could see the glimmer of her mother's cross.

Guilt, fear, shame left him as her eyes met his.

Sophie walked and then, as her father let go of her arm, she ran—those last few steps she ran—to the shield of his arms and the freedom they afforded her.

To him.

Luka kissed the bride before the service had even started.

They needed that moment even if it made the priest cough.

'You're here,' he said.

'So are you.'

'Always.'

Paulo stood, even though he was offered a seat. Luka turned just once and his eyes met Angela's and thanked her.

She, he was sure, was the one who had told the rest of the townsfolk to give these people the chance they deserved and to forgive Paulo now, while they still could.

Their vows were heartfelt.

'I love you,' Luka said. 'I always have and I always will.'

'I love you,' came Sophie's response. 'I always have and I always will.' Then she deviated from the priest's words for she made a small addition. 'And I shall *try* to remember that in all that I say and do.'

No one understood why the groom laughed.

Matteo was the perfect groomsman, even if cynicism was written all over his face, for just yesterday Luka had told him this wedding would never take place, that it was a sham.

But for now he went along with it and handed over the rings.

And tried not to glance at the bridesmaid!

Luka slid on the ring and then he too deviated from tradition, for he went into this pocket and took out another ring and placed it next on her finger.

It was rose gold and the diamond was emerald cut and stood high, and Bella stared at it for a moment, her eyes filling with tears.

She remembered staring in Giovanni's window and a diamond catching her eye.

The hope that when Luka got out, that one day...

There wasn't time to dwell on it for now.

They were man and wife.

The church bells were ringing loudly in Bordo Del Cielo today and as they stepped out, it was to a *true* Sicilian celebration.

The street was lined with tables and dressed in ribbons and flowers, the trees were lit with lights that would glow brighter as evening fell.

Angela and an old friend were helping Paulo out of the church.

'Dance with your father,' Luka said.

She did.

And to hear him laughing and proud was the best medicine for both of them…but then she was back to Luka's arms.

She glanced over his shoulder and smiled. Bella and Matteo were dancing a duty dance, not that it looked like duty for Bella—her eyes were closed and her head was resting on his chest. Only Matteo looked as if he was struggling.

'He's angry,' Luka said. 'He thinks that she is still…' He looked down at Sophie. 'I want to catch up on all the years we have missed, I want to know everything.'

'You shall.'

'Your father is so happy.'

'He wants us to have a baby now.' Sophie smiled.

'You could lie and say you are…'

'Knowing him, he would live for another nine

months just to make sure that we were telling the truth.'

'We are,' Luka said. 'This is for ever.'

'That ring?' Sophie asked. 'Is it from Giovanni's?'

Luka nodded. 'As soon as I got out of court I went and bought it. I wanted to take you to London, not as a friend or a date. Those months in prison had taught me many things…'

Sophie could hardly stand to think of all she had dismissed that day, all the foolish pride she had held onto just to be right.

'I can afford something nicer now.' Luka offered.

'Nothing could be nicer,' Sophie said. 'It belongs with me.'

'So do you.'

EPILOGUE

SOPHIE LAY IN that delicious place between sleep and waking and for a moment she thought she was dreaming.

The lap of the sea, the slow motion of rising and falling with the waves, and Sophie knew she was awake.

She was on honeymoon with Luka.

They were taking their time to sail from Corsica to the Greek islands, stopping where they chose to and just enjoying the journey.

Life was better than she had ever dreamed it might be.

It had been an emotional time. Her father had held on long enough to know that Sophie was expecting a baby. He had seen a summer and a winter in his beloved town and finally he now lay with Rosa.

Sophie lay there thinking about the past months.

It had been Sophie who had thrown her mother's necklace in the grave. It was her mother's, not hers.

She didn't want to wear it day in, day out.

Instead, she wore her mother's earrings, for they spoke of the happiest days with Luka.

And there had been so many of them.

Yes, she was stubborn, but never about that.

'Morning,' Luka said.

'Where were you?'

'Thinking,' he said. 'About us. Are you happy?'

'So happy.' she said, and then looked into his navy eyes. 'And cross with myself for all the time we wasted.'

'We needed that time,' Luka interrupted. 'We were young, there was a lot of pain and little of it was of our making.'

'Even so.'

'We know that what we have is precious,' he said, and she nodded. 'Had I married you when you were nineteen you might have always resented that you never got to work on the cruise liners.'

'No.'

'Yes.'

He smiled and always it made her stomach fold over and in on itself. He was so stern and serious with others, but so open with her.

'And had we got together after the court case and then later found that chain...' Luka thought about it. 'I needed to find out about my father away from you.' It was Luka who brought the name up at times and he was so grateful that her eyes didn't flash in anger; instead, they could hold his gaze as they explored the pains of the past. 'This is our time.'

'So you don't think I was wrong?'

'Sophie...'

'I didn't make us waste all those years?'

'Sophie,' he warned, but he was smiling. 'Come on, let's go and see the sunrise.'

'No, come back to bed,' she grumbled, but Luka shook his head and she got out of bed, put on her sarong and tied it then headed up to the deck.

The sky was gorgeous and just dipping out of navy and the stars were fading.

'Where are we?' Sophie asked, and then she paused as for the first time she saw her home from the sea.

The sun was rising over Sicily and their yacht was close enough that she could make out the familiar landscape—the church where they had not only married but where both their parents rested. She could make out Luka's home, the beach where they had made love.

'I used to sit there every day with Bella,' Sophie said. 'Dreaming of the future, wondering what our lives would be like. I used to picture myself on a cruise liner out on the seas...'

'And now here you are.'

'I'm here with you,' Sophie said, and then she told him a deeper truth, one she hadn't told Bella. Not because she was scared to, she simply hadn't dared admit it to herself, for it had seemed pointless that long-ago day.

'Even though I didn't want to be married, I wanted you then. I wanted it all, I just didn't know how it could happen. How I could be out on the ocean and sailing the seas and somehow be with the man I loved. Yet here I am.'

'We can dock,' Luka said. 'Spend a couple of days there if you wish.'

Sophie thought about it. The people would make them more than welcome. They had their homes back and Bordo Del Cielo was thriving now.

Yet there was no need to go back, no need to visit.

Not now

One day maybe.

They were having a daughter, and they would take her back and, far more gently than they both had, she would learn about her past, about the pain and the beauty of the land that ran through her veins.

But not now.

Now, as Bordo Del Cielo awoke, it was Sophie and Luka that were the glint of a boat on the horizon.

They were out there, together, and living their dreams.

* * * * *

MILLS & BOON®
Large Print – November 2015

The Ruthless Greek's Return
Sharon Kendrick

Bound by the Billionaire's Baby
Cathy Williams

Married for Amari's Heir
Maisey Yates

A Taste of Sin
Maggie Cox

Sicilian's Shock Proposal
Carol Marinelli

Vows Made in Secret
Louise Fuller

The Sheikh's Wedding Contract
Andie Brock

A Bride for the Italian Boss
Susan Meier

The Millionaire's True Worth
Rebecca Winters

The Earl's Convenient Wife
Marion Lennox

Vettori's Damsel in Distress
Liz Fielding

MILLS & BOON®
Large Print – December 2015

The Greek Demands His Heir
Lynne Graham

The Sinner's Marriage Redemption
Annie West

His Sicilian Cinderella
Carol Marinelli

Captivated by the Greek
Julia James

The Perfect Cazorla Wife
Michelle Smart

Claimed for His Duty
Tara Pammi

The Marakaios Baby
Kate Hewitt

Return of the Italian Tycoon
Jennifer Faye

His Unforgettable Fiancée
Teresa Carpenter

Hired by the Brooding Billionaire
Kandy Shepherd

A Will, a Wish...a Proposal
Jessica Gilmore